Jade Summers, mystery woman, manages to steal millionaire's heart....

Former office worker and simple art student manages to net New York's biggest fish....

The newspaper article was short and scandalously to the point.

Jade took a few deep breaths. "Do you have any idea how this ludicrous rumor started?"

Curtis shrugged eloquently. "Getting into a state about it isn't going to change anything."

"I had no idea you were notorious enough to feature in the *gossip columns*," Jade informed him tartly.

Another expressive shrug. "I'm rich, eligible..."

CATHY WILLIAMS is Trinidadian and was brought up on the twin islands of Trinidad and Tobago. She was awarded a scholarship to study in Britain, and came to Exeter University in 1975 to continue her studies into the great loves of her life: languages and literature. It was there that Cathy met her husband, Richard. Since they married, Cathy has lived in England, originally in the Thames Valley but now in the Midlands. Cathy and Richard have three small daughters.

Don't miss any of our special offers. Write to us at the following address for information on our newest releases.

Harlequin Reader Service
U.S.: 3010 Walden Ave., P.O. Box 1325, Buffalo, NY 14269
Canadian: P.O. Box 609, Fort Erie, Ont. L2A 5X3

Cathy Williams

A SCANDALOUS ENGAGEMENT

TORONTO • NEW YORK • LONDON
AMSTERDAM • PARIS • SYDNEY • HAMBURG
STOCKHOLM • ATHENS • TOKYO • MILAN • MADRID
PRAGUE • WARSAW • BUDAPEST • AUCKLAND

ISBN 0-373-12184-9

A SCANDALOUS ENGAGEMENT

First North American Publication 2001.

Copyright © 2000 by Cathy Williams.

Printed in U.S.A.

CHAPTER ONE

'So, you're up at last. I didn't want to disturb you before I left, but have you remembered that the plumber's coming?'

Jade crooked the telephone receiver between her cheek and her shoulder and carried on making herself a cup of coffee. Even after six weeks it still felt decadent to be wandering around this kitchen at nine-thirty in the morning, wearing only her usual garb of jeans and tee shirt. She should be at work. That was always the first thought that sprang into her head when she blearily opened her eyes to peer at the clock at the side of the bed. The clock which no longer summoned her peremptorily out of sleep at six-thirty in the morning with an insistent, aggravating beeping that could raise the dead.

She should be at work. She should be feeling the pressure, because pressure was the only thing that could rescue her from her thoughts. She should be scrambling into her suit and hurrying out of the flat with her bag slung over one shoulder and her briefcase in her hand. She should be preparing for her daily battle with the London Underground, easing her frantic pace only to stop at the news vendor just outside her office block so that she could buy a tabloid to read at lunchtime.

'Of course I've remembered that the plumber's coming.'

The voice down the other end of the telephone laughed warmly. 'I can tell from your tone of voice that you'd forgotten. Two o'clock this afternoon.'

'Oh, very optimistic, your precision.' She poured some

5

milk into her mug and sat down at the kitchen table which, after their initial attempts to keep it free from clutter, now sported enough artist's materials to start a small cottage industry. 'Didn't your mother ever tell you that plumbers have a different sense of time keeping to all other mortals?'

She sipped her coffee, smiling contentedly at the sound of Andy's voice. How did he do that? How did he manage to make her feel so loved and wanted and secure? She had known him for less than a year, but it almost felt as though she had known him for ever. As though he was somehow *meant* to be a part of her life. One of the first things her counsellor had told her was that she needed to begin to trust, needed to stop feeling guilty. Had Andy just happened to come along at the right time, when she'd been beginning the difficult, painful process of chipping her barriers away? Was that why she felt so close to him? As though he was the soulmate she had been blindly searching for over the past two years?

'No,' Andy said thoughtfully down the line. 'Amongst her erratically scattered pearls of wisdom, advice concerning plumbers was noticeably absent. Do you think that's been part of my problem?'

He chuckled softly, and Jade felt a rush of pleasure at his words. Over the past few months he had opened up in ways neither of them would have thought possible. Both of them had. They had tentatively shared the common ground of counselling, learning to expose their fears and voice their nightmares, and it had paid off. They had learned to reach out to each other, and if she still didn't automatically react with trust to most people, she was getting better.

'Now, *there's* a possibility,' Jade joked back, her eyes skimming over some work she had started the day before and liking what she saw. 'Okay, I'll make sure I'm washed and brushed by two, even though I'd bet you ten quid that the man doesn't show up on time. He'll stroll in just as we're about to sit down and eat dinner and rake up a few limp excuses about "burst water pipes, guv."'

'That's more than possible, but got to keep the old place ticking over.'

'Don't I know it.' There had been an unspoken acceptance between them from the start that sharing this house involved a complicated series of unwritten rules and regulations. No clutter. No mess. Definitely no broken appliances left to go rusty. And top of the list was 'No Leaks'. Leaking water could destroy wallpaper and ruin all the tasteful silk that seemed to thread through each of the impressive rooms, not to mention wreak havoc with the paintings.

The paintings, Andy had told her before she had moved in, were worth a small fortune, but she had still been unprepared for the quantity of them. Picassos were dotted about the house with the casual ease that typified people for whom money was no object. She had spent her first day just wandering through the graceful house, nestled in a secluded spot just outside central London, amazed at the profuse splendour while Andy had trailed behind her, smiling indulgently at her gasps of awe.

The place, which he contemptuously referred to as the Mausoleum, was a testament to well-bred opulence. Nothing was overdone but everything had clearly been chosen with no thought of cost. And, however bitterly he spoke of the background that had failed him, he still fitted in: blond, elegant and as beautiful as any Adonis that had been tenderly crafted by its sculptor.

Even now, having grown accustomed to all of it, she still found herself wondering what it must have been like to have been brought up amidst such splendour. A house in the country, another in the wilds of Scotland, yet another in the South of France. The holidays in far-flung places. She imagined his parents, now dead for many years, as a glorious, golden couple. She had spotted pictures of them in the house and her imagination had taken flight at the images of his mother, the typical blonde, English rose, and his father, the typical debonair, dark Greek tycoon. It seemed somehow tragic that all their son could resurrect from his childhood memories was a legacy of nannies, a loathing of boarding schools and a glimpse of his beautiful parents in between their endless and impressive social engagements.

From what she had gathered over time, his had been a life of loneliness and absentee parents, who had compensated for their shortcomings with lavish gifts and money. She pictured him, and his two siblings, rattling around in all those huge houses with a wake of well-paid nannies in attendance, waiting for the hour when their glamorous parents would pay them a brief night-time visit for the statutory peck on the cheek and a quick inspection to make sure that nothing was visibly amiss and the nannies were doing what they were paid for.

Andy Greene had been an emotional mess waiting to happen. She was only glad that their separate chaotic personal troubles had led them to one another.

Two hours after the phone call, Jade had completely forgotten the plumber.

She was still at the table in the kitchen, the only room in the house where disorder was allowed because there were no priceless furnishings that could be accidentally damaged, her slim fingers skimming over the paper in front of her as she experimented with various layouts for a children's book. She was becoming more confident by the day. It had made no difference that she had studied art at college for two years after leaving school. All that had been years ago, and the first time she had re-entered the art school in London she had been as nervous as if she had never glimpsed the inside of one in her life before. She had stared at pastels and paintbrushes and cartridge paper with the fear of someone suddenly crippled by stage fright. But time was beginning to do its thing. Time and the talent which she had thought had been abandoned for ever by the wayside when all her dreams had turned sour.

She sat back, frowning, and gazed at what she had accomplished over the past few days. The illustrations were lively, but they lacked detail. No matter. She would go back over them and painstakingly begin to put the detail in. It was the bit she loved most. The loving strokes that turned the sketches into the finely etched drawings which she would then paint over in watercolour. She bent her head so that her shoulder-length buttermilk-blonde hair dipped across her face and was raising her hand to begin her work when the doorbell went.

For half a minute she chose to ignore it, but when the ringing turned into banging she distantly remembered the wretched plumber and reluctantly dropped her pencil and walked to the front door.

Of course the damned man would choose this very minute to pay his visit. Well ahead of the time he had given them. Wasn't that just typical? Jade thought irritably, gritting her teeth together. Hadn't she said that they operated in another hemisphere when it came to time?

'All right!' she yelled, when one bang threatened to bring the door down. Whoever was hammering on the door was certainly no small, retiring type. 'I'm coming!'

She worked her way through the three locks and yanked open the door, scowling in anticipation of the brute on the other side. Her chocolate-brown eyes were confronted by a chest and, as they quickly travelled upwards, by the most powerfully impressive man she had ever set eyes on before in her life.

He was swarthy, and something about the set of his features and the angular planes of his face lifted him from the merely handsome into the realm of dangerously sensual. His thick hair was very dark, almost black, and in contrast his blue eyes were the ice-blue colour of the sky in winter. She felt an instant and fleeting jolt of unaccustomed awareness surge through her like a sudden electric shock, and she almost took a step backwards, surprised and unsettled by her reaction.

She was still scowling furiously as she met his eyes, though, and was incensed to see that he was scowling back at her. The nerve! So plumbers were in short supply, but who did this one think he was?

She also noted, in passing, that he was not dressed in plumber's overalls. Not unless plumber's garb in London ran along the lines of a trench coat with cream-coloured wool jumper and khaki trousers. Good grief. She only hoped that he hadn't come out to inspect the site and was considering sending in one of his chaps at a later date. Last seen, the leak in Andy's bedroom had been dripping slowly but persistently into a saucepan which they had strategically placed underneath and had shown no signs of letting up.

'Good of you to answer the door,' the man said coldly. 'Didn't you hear the doorbell first time around?'

Jade was almost too angry to speak coherently. She stuck her hand on one slim hip and gave him a withering look which failed to do the trick.

'You're early,' she said, through gritted teeth. 'And I was busy in the kitchen.'

'I'm *early*?' For a second the scowl disappeared, replaced by a look of astonishment which only managed to make him look more aggressively good-looking, then he

was scowling again, this time with somewhat more inso-
lence, allowing his eyes to rake over her and making no
attempt to conceal the fact.

Jade abruptly turned away. This was the last thing she
was in line for. A lecherous plumber with the manners of
a warthog and enough of an over-sized ego to consider
himself above overalls and tool kit.

'You'd better come in,' she said, not that he was standing
on ceremony by waiting outside. Oh, no, he was stepping
right through the front door, wet shoes and all. 'And wipe
your feet,' she ordered. 'You're not dripping mud into this
house. In fact, you might as well take your shoes off and
leave them by the door.' She gave his shoes a scathing look
and was frustrated but not surprised to see that they were
as out of character as the rest of his outfit. She was no
connoisseur of men's shoes, but these didn't look as though
they had spent their lifetime being dragged through mud.

'Just exactly *who* are you?' he asked, looking at her nar-
rowly and not, she noticed, removing his shoes.

'Jade Summers,' Jade replied, bristling. 'And in case the
name doesn't ring a bell, I'm the person you've come to
see about this plumbing job.' She looked him squarely in
the face, which necessitated her straining her neck upwards
because frankly, to her five foot six, the man was a hulking
giant.

'Plumbing job.' He continued to stare at her, then he
stroked his chin thoughtfully with one finger.

'Ah! So you remember, do you?' she said sarcastically.
'Andy, Mr Greene, got in touch with you last night to come
and mend a leak?'

'A leak...'

'Would you mind not repeating everything I say?' She
flashed him another of her specialty cold, quenching smiles
which, again, had no effect. 'And I'm beginning to doubt

whether you're competent to handle the job, Mr...' He inclined his head to one side while she tried to rack her brains for the name Andy had tossed at her at eleven-thirty the night before. 'Mr Wilkins. You're hardly dressed appropriately, and you don't seem to know anything about leaks. Shouldn't you be asking a few pertinent questions by now? Like *Where exactly is your leak, madam?* Or *Perhaps you'd care to wait while I just fetch my tools?*' She folded her arms and looked at him with narrow-eyed suspicion. 'I take it you *are* a qualified plumber...?'

'I have lots of qualifications,' the man replied coolly, outstaring her so that she was forced to look away.

'Good.' She knew he had. Andy had randomly picked one from the *Yellow Pages* with the biggest advertising space and she vaguely recalled seeing a few letters here and there after his name. 'In that case...' She eyed the trench coat. 'Maybe you'd like to divest yourself of your coat and follow me upstairs.'

'*Divest?* That's a complicated word for... I beg your pardon. I got the name, but not what your position is here...'

He didn't *sound* like a plumber either. Not that she had any idea what plumbers sounded like, since she had never, fortunately, had to cross paths with one. This specimen was obviously a university-educated one, hence the arrogance.

'That's because I didn't mention it, and it's none of your business anyway. You just need to know that I'm in charge.' She couldn't believe she had just said that. Firm she could be, and had had to be for years, working as personal assistant, first of all, then upward bound until she had virtually been all but running the small company she had worked for ever since she'd moved to London two and a half years previously. But *tyrannical?* Never in a million years.

But what other way to go was there in this situation? Whether this Wilkins man was the boss of his own company or merely an employee with an over-inflated sense of himself, he needed a bit of discipline.

'Follow me,' she ordered, looking at his stylish and, more ominously, clean clothes in a jaundiced way. She would give him the benefit of the doubt, but if he had come prepared to fix a leaking ceiling, then she would eat her hat. If she'd possessed one. And there was no point asking her to lead him to the nearest spanner, or whatever tools he needed, because she had no idea where she would find any in the house, and she was pretty certain that Andy would be as clueless as herself.

'The leak's in one of the bedrooms,' she explained, ahead of him, uneasily aware of his presence behind her. She hoped to high heaven that she wouldn't be subjected to another of his all-over inspections or worse. She shivered, and mentally called up his face, all brooding, dark sensuality. The sort of face that women swooned over. Was straightforward plumbing all he did when he went to houses to mend leaks, or was he accustomed to women giving him the come-on?

She decided to let him go ahead of her. It paid to be careful.

'The bedroom's just down there,' she told him, standing back and pointing along the corridor.

'Just down *where*?'

'Last door on the left. You can't miss it. We had to pull the bed out and stick a container under the leak to catch the water.' She watched him warily as he sauntered along the corridor, looking through the open doors, in no visible hurry to get to his destination.

'And would you mind hurrying up?' she called after him impatiently. 'I have a lot of chores to be going on with.'

'So you work here, do you?' he called back casually, taking his time, as though she hadn't spoken. He paused outside the bedroom door to look at her, hands thrust into the pockets of his trousers. 'Don't you want to come and hear what I've got to report about your leak?' he asked loudly. 'Nothing to be afraid of, *madam*. I'm a perfectly well-behaved member of the human race.'

She didn't like the way he had called her *madam*. It reeked of disrespect. She pursed her lips together and walked towards him.

The man was wasted in his business, she thought absent-mindedly. He was just too predatorial-looking to spend his life peering down broken drains and inspecting faulty washing machines. He should be out in a jungle somewhere, exploring the depths of the Amazon and slaying man-eating snakes with his bare hands. Or something like that.

'It's over the bed. There.' She pointed to the ceiling and the patch of wallpaper underneath which had been unravelled by the dripping water.

'I see.' He walked into the room, side-stepping various articles of clothing which were lying on the ground.

'Andy's room,' she found herself saying, just in case he thought that this mess belonged to her. At the age of twenty-two, and four years her junior, Andy still hadn't developed any noticeable talent for clearing up behind him. Twice a week a cleaner came and purged the house, but in the intervening days he allowed his bedroom to develop the sort of teenage chaos that would have driven most mothers round the twist. She supposed that his untidiness was simply a reflection of the fact that he had never had the need to be tidy. There had always been someone else clearing up behind him, making sure that everything was neatly folded and put away. Even when he cooked, which he did with flourish, the kitchen afterwards resembled a badly bombed site.

She edged over the wrought-iron bedframe and snatched a pair of boxer shorts off it, dropping them to the ground and then kicking them under the bed. When she raised her eyes, it was to find the plumber looking at her with an unreadable expression.

'You were saying about the leak?' she reminded him weakly, staring in concentration at the damp patch on the ceiling.

'Could be serious.'

Jade's face blanched. 'Serious? How serious?' She didn't like the sound of that. It didn't look like much from where she was standing, but then again she wasn't a plumber, and who knew what build-up of water could be lurking above the ceiling? She imagined Niagara Falls pouring down the wall, destroying everything in its wake, including the vastly expensive carpeting.

'Can't be sure.' He stroked his chin again and continued to stare at her, which she failed to notice with the onset of the horrific, water-filled scenario that was now running through her head. 'You say you…what?…spotted the water…?'

'We were watching television and I felt a drip on my head,' Jade explained, dragging her eyes away from the ceiling and meeting his, which were now glacial. 'Andy got on the phone immediately,' she said defensively, primed to contradict any accusations of irresponsibility, not that it should be any concern of the man in front of her. 'I was here when he made the call, and I *know* that he stressed the importance of getting it seen to as soon as possible.'

'And what time would that have been?'

'A little after eleven in the night,' Jade said impatiently.

'Don't you people keep a log book or something for in-coming calls? Look, can you fix it or not?'

'Not at the moment.'

Jade groaned in despair. 'But we—Andy *explained* to you the importance of getting this sorted out. Yet you come here without so much as a screwdriver in sight and tell me that you can't fix it at the moment.' She sat on the edge of the bed. 'Well, when *can* you fix it?'

'Why don't we go downstairs to discuss this?'

'What's there to discuss?' It seemed perfectly clear-cut to her.

'What needs to be done.' He shrugged and continued to look at her with relentless concentration. She could almost hear his brain ticking away in his head. Probably working out the vast charges he would make at the end of this little job.

'Oh, all right.' She stood up wearily, threw one last disgusted look at the leak, which appeared so inoffensive, or had done until the Wilkins man had said otherwise, and headed out of the room.

'Perhaps we could discuss the situation over a cup of coffee,' he suggested to her, halfway down the stairs, and she paused to look at him over her shoulder.

'Haven't you got other jobs you need to get to?'

'Not at the moment.' He had stopped when she had turned to address him. Now he took another step down, and for some reason the thought of being cooped up on the staircase with this man towering over her was enough to get her legs moving again. She swung around, trailing her hand along the banister, and skipped lightly down the remainder of the stairs.

'Well, *I* happen to be quite busy,' she said pointedly, leading the way to the kitchen.

'Of course. Doing what?'

'I beg your pardon?' She couldn't believe her ears. The man's rudeness defied description.

'I only ask because I've been here before. A few times, actually, and the house has been empty.'

'Why would a plumber come to an empty house?'

'Contract.' He shrugged eloquently, as though that single word explained a host of things.

Jade groped her way to further enlightenment. 'Oh, I get it. You come every so often to check up on the place and make sure that everything's running smoothly?'

'Exactly.'

'I'm surprised Andy didn't recognise your name in the book, in that case,' she mused aloud, filling the kettle with water and plugging it in.

'We plumbers. A forgetful lot.' He raised his eyebrows expressively, and somewhere in the depths of her head she realised that he was laughing at her.

'Yes. Quite. How do you take your coffee?'

'Black, one sugar. So...' He strolled around the kitchen and finally, as she had known he would, ambled over to the kitchen table, where he looked with interest at the drawings spread across the wooden surface. From the other end of the room, Jade watched him with a growing feeling of antagonism.

'Have a seat, Mr Wilkins,' she said tightly, 'and then perhaps we could discuss the matter at hand?'

'Draw, do you?'

'That's right, and I really haven't got the time for chit-chat.' How much more blatant did she have to be? She filled their mugs with boiling water, wondered whether it was too late to call in another firm to have a look at the leak, and then stood stock still as he held up one of her sketches to the light and began inspecting it.

'You do this professionally, do you?' he asked, depositing the sheet of paper and replacing it with another, which he held up and inspected with the same thorough eye.

'I'm an art student, as a matter of fact,' Jade told him icily. She dumped his mug of coffee on the counter, directed him to it, and then took the opportunity to stack away some of her work, aware of him looking at her as she did so, leaning against the counter, utterly at ease.

'You're an art student. Yes, I see.'

'And what *precisely* do you see, Mr Wilkins? A way to fixing our leak, I hope.'

'Oh, yes, that shouldn't be a big job.'

'I thought you said that it was serious.'

'Did I?'

Jade's teeth snapped together in frustration.

'You know you did.'

'How on earth does an art student come to be living in a house like this?' he asked, deftly avoiding all discussion of what he had come to do.

'I happen to share the place with a friend, as a matter of fact. Now, when can you send someone along to fix this leak?'

'What makes you think that *I* won't be the one to come and fix it myself?'

'Because of your nails, aside from anything else.'

'My nails?' He looked puzzled for a few seconds, then he laughed. It was a distinctive laugh. Deep and sexy, with enough wickedness in it to turn grannies into simpering adolescents. 'Ah, yes. Not dirty enough?'

'Put it this way, Mr Wilkins, you don't strike me as the sort of man who's ever changed a car tyre in his life, never mind peered into the innards of a drainpipe. Now, why don't we stop beating around the bush. Just tell me whom I can expect, when, and how much you intend to charge for your services.'

She wondered why she hadn't seen through his ploy before. Wasn't it as plain as the nose on her face? Mr Heart-Stopping Big Boss makes initial appearance, charms lady of the house into winning a job which inevitably would be much smaller than he makes out, then sends his troops in with outsized invoice in hand. Probably ran a very thriving business indeed. No wonder he could afford to dress the way he did.

Unfortunately for him, *she* wasn't in the running for good looks and cheap charm. She had never been tempted by handsome men with a sweet tongue. No, that had been her sister's domain.

She felt the familiar pain rush into her and rested her head momentarily against the palm of her hand. When she regained her composure, it was to find the man looking at her with sudden concern.

'Are you all right?'

'Fine.' She didn't feel fine. She felt sick, just as she always did whenever she thought of Caroline. 'Just a passing headache,' she said shakily. 'Must be all that detailed work I've been doing recently.'

'You look as though you've seen a ghost.'

The remark was so accurate that Jade stared at him open-mouthed, then she blinked and shook her head. Yes, she *had* seen a ghost in a manner of speaking. A little over two years and the image of her sister still haunted her. All that promise sucked away at the age of twenty-four. She had a sudden, overwhelming temptation to bare her soul to this complete stranger sitting opposite her, frowning now, and she had to bite it back.

Yes, her counsellor had said that she couldn't hold on to the past for ever; yes, she had said that she should learn to talk to people about how she felt, to cherish the life that she had known instead of allowing it to ruin her own life.

But she was in a bad way if that meant pouring her heart out to a con man whom she had spoken with for all of an hour. If that.

'I think it's time you left,' she said, making a half-hearted attempt to rise to her feet and then sinking back to the stabilising comfort of the kitchen chair. 'I…Andy will telephone you later to sort out…everything.'

'You're beginning to worry me, Miss Summers.'

'I'm fine.'

'Perhaps I should get you upstairs.'

'Don't be ridiculous.' She was feeling faint again. In an effort to dispel his unwanted concern, she stood up and felt herself sway, then, before she knew it, he had moved swiftly around the table and lifted her off her feet.

'What are you doing! Put me down *this instant*.'

'Forget it. I'm not going to be responsible for leaving you in this house. What if you collapse the minute I leave?'

'I don't intend to do any such thing! Put me down!' This was a nightmare. One minute she was contentedly working away at the kitchen table; the next minute she was being carried upstairs by the local plumber, who apparently thought that she was ill and needed immediate rescue! It was farcical! She continued to demand instant release until he got to the top of the stairs, then she gave up. He was bigger than her, stronger than her, and determined to do his hero bit. Well, let him.

He began heading towards Andy's room and she feebly told him that he was going in the wrong direction.

'I thought your bedroom was down there, leaking from the seams,' he said.

'No. Mine's in the other direction, second from the right.' She could smell him through his shirt, feel the hardness of his chest against her cheek. Everything about him was unashamedly masculine, she thought, from his powerful, well-built body to the way he smelled. She couldn't wait to get away from the experience.

'I do apologise,' he said, without a hint of apology in his voice. 'I must have misunderstood.'

'I'm not interested in your misunderstandings, Mr Wilkins.' Her bedroom door was getting closer and she breathed a sigh of relief. If Caroline were alive now, she would be grinning with merriment at the sight of her shy twin sister being manhandled by just the sort of hulk she had always made a point of avoiding. For the first time she felt a rush of affectionate memories for her sister without any of the accompanying loss and guilt.

He kicked open her bedroom door and Jade peeked to make sure that there was nothing unfortunate lying around. Like her bra. It was spotless, just as she had left it earlier on. The bed carefully made, her clothes tidied away. Andy always laughed at her neatness, but now she couldn't have been more grateful for it.

'Just dump me on the bed,' she instructed. 'Then you can go. I won't bother to see you out. Just slam the door behind you.'

He didn't answer. He deposited her on the bed, stood up, looked around the room with the same practised eye she had seen in evidence earlier, and then returned his gaze to her face.

'You're already looking better.'

She knew why. The colour had returned to her cheeks because she was flushed from the feel of his arms around her. The thought was enough to make her even redder.

'I'll just have a short rest here and I'll be as fit as a fiddle.' She wished he would exit her bedroom, instead of standing there looking at her. Not that she had any feeling of being mentally stripped. Despite her initial worry that she might be dealing with a tedious lecher, he was not sexually interested in her. When he looked at her it was almost as though he was working something out in his head, although that could be just her imagination playing tricks on her.

And, frankly, why should he be interested in her? He was, she reluctantly had to admit, an unusually attractive man, and she was, if she was honest, attractive enough, but hardly a Marilyn Monroe. Her hair was blonde, but straight, her features were small, but unextraordinary, and she was way too slender and flat-chested to ever be termed voluptuous. Her sister's body had been the one that men had flocked to. More rounded, fuller everywhere, and with the good legs which they had both inherited from their mother. She had flaunted it at every available opportunity. Jade sighed and leant back against the pillows.

'Do you want a cup of tea or anything?'

Jade gave him a saccharine-sweet smile. 'I really don't think so. You wouldn't have a clue where to find anything, it's not your house, and anyway cups of sweet tea don't actually cure anything. It's all a myth.'

'You're probably right,' he agreed. 'So this is where you sleep?'

'Goodbye.'

He continued to survey her room critically. 'No television. Is that why you were in the other bedroom at that hour of the evening?'

'You,' Jade said furiously, 'are totally out of order. What I do in this house is none of your business. You came here to fix a leak, which you aren't even competent enough to do, and if you don't leave immediately I shall...'

'Throw me out by the scruff of my neck?'

This situation, she thought, was getting out of hand. He was beginning to frighten her a little now.

'Let's put it this way; there are other plumbers around. Now, please *go*!'

'Oh, I don't think so.' He sat on the edge of the bed and Jade squirmed into a sitting position, drawing her legs up and clasping her arms around them. She looked desperately towards the door, wondering whether she could make a dash for it. But if he wanted to he would have no trouble in pinning her down.

'Get out or else I'm going to call the police.' Quiet, menacing, utterly serious. He failed to be intimidated.

'That won't work either, you know,' he said conversationally.

'Want to bet?'

'I don't take money off a lady, if that's what you are.' He inclined his body forward slightly. 'Nor do I wrest telephones away from people, if that's what you're thinking. No, it won't make any difference *who* you call...'

'And why not?'

'Because I'm Andy's brother and I own this house.'

CHAPTER TWO

'I DON'T believe you.'

She did. Something hadn't added up from the minute she had laid eyes on him. His clothes, his accent, his general charisma. But she had been expecting a plumber and she had naively assumed that because he had showed up he *must* be the plumber she had been waiting for. Of course, she should have asked for his card instead of innocently running with her assumptions while he played along, trying to pump information out of her all the way.

Too late now.

'Of course you believe me,' he said coldly. 'But just in case there are any lingering doubts in your mind...' He extracted a wallet from his trouser pocket, flicked it open to reveal a row of platinum and gold credit cards, and extracted his driver's licence from one of the compartments.

Jade dutifully took it, confirmed his identity and handed it back to him.

She couldn't think of a thing to say. She knew why he had come, and Andy was going to be distraught.

'Cat got your tongue, Miss Summers? I'm disappointed. You were so eloquent up to ten minutes ago.'

Jade glared at him with loathing. 'Why didn't you just introduce yourself at the front door and spare us both the ludicrous pretence?'

'Now, why on earth should I have done that?' He stuck his wallet away and proceeded to view her without warmth. 'I didn't know who the hell you were, but I was willing to stake my fortune on your not being the daily help, and you

24

would have clamped up the minute you knew who I was. No, it was altogether far more productive for me to go along with the charade and see what I could find out along the way.' He stood up, strolled across to the bay window and looked out before turning around. 'You look as though you could do with a stiff drink,' he said in a deceptively mild voice. 'Don't go fainting on me, now. I have too many questions to ask.' He smiled with dangerous menace. 'And far too many answers you're just bursting to give.'

'I'll get in touch with Andy,' she said, reaching across to the telephone at the side of her bed, but before she could pick up the receiver his hand was over hers like a vice, stopping her.

'Not so fast, Miss Summers. You're in *my* house and you're going to listen to what *I* have to say. Do you read me loud and clear? And we'll just wait for my brother to return. I'm sure he'd far rather appreciate the surprise.'

'Your hand? Please remove it. I don't appreciate the caveman approach.'

Another of those deep, velvety, unsettling laughs, but he removed his hand and stood back.

'A girl with spirit. Unusual for my brother.'

'And what is *that* supposed to mean?' Jade asked quickly, shooting back to the furthest edge of the bed just in case he got it into his head to try another lunge at her. The man seemed to have a bad effect on her nervous system, and she was rapidly discovering that the closer he got, the worse the effect was.

'It means that the few trollops he's ever had, *to my knowledge*, have all been watery, insignificant bores with the personalities of wet rags.'

Jade sighed. She had never thought that she would meet Curtis Greene. When she and Andy had moved into his house he had assured her that his brother was a workaholic, firmly ensconced in the fast-living bowels of Manhattan, and rarely came to London. When he did there would be advance notice, and they would simply move out until he had cleared off.

He clearly disliked his older brother, even though she had detected a certain awe and admiration in his voice whenever his name was mentioned, and conversations about him had been limited.

'So I think it's question-and-answer time, Miss Summers, don't you?' No wonder he had failed to be intimidated by her withering looks, she thought miserably. Lord of the house and master of the withering look, himself. The sort of man who would fail to be intimidated by a charging rhino, never mind a diminutive blonde with more lip than common sense.

'And, charming though the bedroom is, I don't think it's quite the place for a conversation.' He began walking towards the door, looking around only when he was standing in the doorway. 'Why don't we adjourn to the sitting room? We'll be far more comfortable there. Unless, of course, you're the sort who finds bedrooms the best place to be...?'

Jade sprang out of the bed, barely sparing him a glance, her arms protectively folded across her chest, and brushed past him, irritated to find that, despite his high-handed, despicable, loathsome arrogance, she still found that fleeting physical contact with his shirt slightly unnerving.

'I don't care *who* you are,' was her opening shot, as soon as they were in the sitting room, 'I don't like your attitude. You may think it's a whizz threatening people but it won't work on me. And rubbing my nose in the fact that this is *your* house and I'm a *trespasser* isn't going to work either. I have no problem with packing up my things and moving out.'

Her bank manager might find it a little worrying, she

thought, but she had enough money saved from her last job to see her through finding a place to rent. And working while she studied was hardly inconceivable. The offer from Andy to share this house, with space for her to paint and only their bills and food to cover, had been manna from heaven, but if it involved bowing and scraping to the brute in front of her, then forget it.

'Spirited, and full of indignant, outraged pride,' was his only comment, as he moved to one of the chairs and sat down. Like his brother, Curtis Greene paid scant attention to his surroundings, and, like his brother, he fitted in, from the casual elegance of his clothes to the unspoken assumption of authority he exuded. But unlike his brother, who was a charming and loveable player, Curtis Greene was neither charming nor loveable. He was a shaker and mover whom, she imagined, moved through life playing by his rules and expecting the rest of the world to fall obediently in line.

'Why don't you drop the act, Miss Summers? It's just the two of us now, and we both know what you are.'

Jade tentatively perched on the chair furthest from his and stared at him in bewilderment.

'An art student,' she said after a while.

'So-called.'

'You can telephone the college in London and confirm it,' she told him coldly. 'What do you think I am, if *not* an art student? Do you think that I sit at the kitchen table every morning with a load of phoney drawings scattered around me, idly waiting for someone to drop by so that I can launch into a string of pathological lies?' She gave a short, derisive laugh and his mouth tightened.

'You have a brain and a vocabulary,' he mused aloud. 'Curiouser and curiouser.' He frowned thoughtfully, as though genuinely baffled by the phenomenon, but she wasn't fooled for a minute. This series of observations was all linked to his own agenda, and she was pretty sure that when she discovered what the agenda was she wasn't going to like it.

'Now what *would* my brother see in you?'

Poor Andy, she thought. If he had spent a lifetime coping with this sort of condescending attitude. No wonder the shutters came down every time he mentioned the name Curtis.

'Just get to the point, Mr Greene, so that I can pack my bags and leave.'

'Now, you don't *really* want to do that, do you?'

'Well, no,' Jade agreed, flummoxed. 'But it is *your* house, as you pointed out...'

With a sudden movement he stripped off the thick cream sweater to reveal a checked shirt in muted greens and creams and browns. Very slowly he began to roll back the sleeves, exposing strong forearms, liberally sprinkled with fine, dark hair. Jade watched, mesmerised. For a big man, his movements were as graceful as a cat's.

'How did you meet my brother?' he asked conversationally, pausing briefly to glance in her direction, then sitting back in the chair, his head tilted backwards so that his eyes became narrowed, watchful slits.

Had Andy mentioned anything to him about the counselling? she wondered. Doubtful. Aside from Christmas cards and the occasional letter, he'd said that their communications had always been restricted to faxes and E-mails about the company.

'Oh, we met through mutual friends,' she said vaguely.

'*What* mutual friends might those be?'

'None that you would know,' she answered shortly.

'So you met and...what? Instantly hit it off? Started dating?'

'We *did* instantly hit it off, yes,' she replied uneasily. She was being led somewhere and she didn't like the feeling. She got the impression that every word she spoke was ensnaring her yet further in whatever ambush he had surreptitiously laid down.

'And then you moved in? I thought Andy refused to have anything to do with this house? Hasn't he got his own flat in the Barbican? And what about you? Where were *you* living?'

'I don't know whether he *refused* to have anything to do with this house or not. He's never spoken to me about that. I just assumed that it was your house and so—'

'He's always known that he can live here whenever he wants to,' he interrupted abruptly. 'My question is *why* has he chosen to move in here now? What's suddenly wrong with his flat?'

'He's lent it out to a friend of your sister who's over here from Australia for six months.'

'Ah, so *Sarah* asked him if he would do her the favour…?'

'And also…'

'Yes?' He looked at her with interest, or at least the interest, she thought darkly, that a shark might show in a prospective meal.

She squared her shoulders and came right out with it. 'When Andy quit his job, we both thought that it might be a nice idea for us to move in here so that we could have more space respectively for our art work. We had no idea that you would be returning to London.'

'So I gather. My apologies if I've broken up the cosy little love-nest.'

Jade went bright red at his words, opened her mouth to contradict him, and then closed it again. She might as well wait for his full sheet of accusations before she started defending herself.

'You must have both known that I'd be back, though. Didn't you?' His mouth curled. 'Did Andy imagine for one second that he could fax me his letter of resignation and get no reaction from me but a good luck card and a transatlantic pat on the shoulder?'

'You'll have to ask your brother that one,' she muttered uncomfortably, shifting in the chair, aware that she was perspiring slightly and highly resenting the way he made her feel, like a criminal being tried for charges as yet unspecified.

'I'm asking *you!*' he exploded, shedding his cool demeanour and giving her a taste of what lay underneath. A dangerous wolf in dangerous wolf's clothing. As if she hadn't already figured that one out. All wolves had teeth and he was baring his.

She steeled herself not to wilt at his outburst and gave him a serene smile.

'Yes, well, there's no need to raise your voice, Mr Greene, and you must know that I can't answer your question, since I don't know what's going on in every recess of your brother's head.'

'Well, answer me this,' he rasped. 'Did you coerce Andy into this move so that you could get your pretty little foot through the door?'

The accusation, thinly disguised as a question, was followed by such a long silence that the soft noises in the room, the gentle ticking of the antique clock on the mantelpiece, became resounding explosions. She felt fury rush through her, and she had to clamp shut her mouth just in case she started yelling at him. Yelling never got anyone anywhere. It just made a situation worse.

'I see where all this is leading. No wonder you didn't

want me to call Andy. You needed a bit of time on your own to try and pin me down into...what, exactly? Breaking down and confessing that I'm a gold-digger who's ruthlessly using your brother for his money?'

'It won't be the first time that a woman's head has been turned by a big bank balance,' he grated, recovering his deadly calm. 'And Andy's a gullible victim. He likes the underdog.'

'I am *not* an underdog, Mr Greene. I happen to have been holding down a very good job before...' She paused, pulling herself sharply back from any mention of counselling. 'Before I decided to go back into art.'

'Which is why it just doesn't add up, if you don't mind my saying.' He gave her a cold, triumphant smile. 'The few girls I have ever known my brother to associate with have all been simpering females without a brain between their ears. You have to admit that it's a bit strange to find him here with you now, cohabiting in the family mansion which he swore he would never return to. I'm not a complete fool, Miss Summers, and I'm nothing like my brother. I've never been taken in by feminine wiles in my entire life and I can smell a scam from a mile away.

'You're clever. Clever enough to interest my brother long enough to get what you want. Did you flatter his ego? Was that how you decided to operate? A cunning word here, a sideways glance there, a soft gasp of admiration when he confided that he had always been interested in the world of art? Was that how it went, Miss Summers? Then a hesitant suggestion that perhaps moving in together might be a good idea? Get to know one another better? Share your love of art at close range? Was that how things progressed?'

Jade's fists clenched into balls at her sides. It was all so ridiculous that she very nearly burst out laughing. If only he knew. But the fact was that Curtis Greene knew nothing at all about his brother. He had never taken the time to find out.

'What's so damned funny?' he asked with narrow-eyed suspicion.

The ghost of a smile which had curved her lips upwards turned into a grin which became even broader as she watched his expression go from hostile suspicion to outright wrath. She began to laugh, throwing her head back and giving full vent to the sound that had become so alien to her over the past two years. She laughed until the tears rolled down her face, and then she subsided into giggles, wiping her eyes with the backs of her hands like a child. Eventually she sobered up enough to look at him.

'I haven't laughed so much in years,' she said in a sudden, confiding outburst. 'Thank you.'

'My pleasure.' There was naked curiosity in the cool blue eyes now, but instead of trying to slake it he lowered his eyes for a few seconds, then returned his gaze to her face.

'But I don't get the joke.'

'The joke, Mr Greene, is not just that you're utterly and hopelessly wrong about me. It's *how* utterly and hopelessly wrong you are. I'm not after your brother's money, or anyone else's money for that matter. I learned the hard way that money doesn't buy anything that really makes a difference.' She paused, shocked that for the second time this aggravating, misguided man had almost succeeded in reaching a place in her that very few people had reached thus far. If any.

'Very philosophical for a girl of…eighteen? Nineteen?'

'Twenty-six, actually.'

'Then *what* is your relationship with my brother?' he demanded.

'What business is it of yours?'

'What business is it of mine? *What business is it of mine?*' he spluttered, wearing the expression of someone who could hardly believe what they were hearing. 'God, woman, you've got some bare-faced cheek!'

'Oh, sorry.' Now that his mask of thunderous wrath had slipped, she allowed herself to relax. The atmosphere had altered between them. She couldn't quite work out *how*, but she suspected that it was because however much his logic tried to tell him that she was up to no good, his instincts were telling him otherwise. And, peripherally, he was not accustomed to being answered back. She sensed that in some strange, intangible way. He was a man who had prematurely assumed a mantle of power and had grown to accept the respect and subservience it would have brought him.

She knew enough from Andy to piece together Curtis Greene in a way she would not have been capable of doing had she simply met him out of the blue. She knew that he had been the first born, the love-child of his parents when his mother had been only a girl herself. The marriage that had ensued had been going for quite some years before two more children had been produced. By the time his parents had died, in a light aircraft accident, Curtis had been a young man in his early twenties, and without warning had found himself catapulted into a dynasty which he had proved himself more than equipped to handle. More importantly, he had found himself surrogate parent to his two younger siblings and, from what she had gathered, had fulfilled his role through the iron rod of discipline rather than the gentle hand of love.

His past had made him the person that he was today, just as it had made his brother the person he had turned out to be.

She found that she was staring at him, mentally trying to piece him together in much the same way he had been trying to piece *her* together earlier on, and she only snapped back to the present when he said roughly, 'He's my brother. I have to look out for him.'

'In which case, you have nothing to fear from me.' She lowered her eyes and half smiled to herself as she played the secrets she held in her head. 'Andy and I are simply very good friends. Two people who get along.'

'I find that difficult to believe.'

'Why? Men and women can have very satisfying relationships that aren't based on...'

'Sex?' He shot her a slow, crooked smile and she felt her breath suddenly quicken. From her previously secure vantage point, she now experienced a disconcerting slip in her mental resources. Something about his smile, the way his mouth curved when he murmured that one word, the sudden change in the tenor of his voice, made the room seem much smaller and very hot.

'Yes. Quite.' She cleared her throat and adopted an expression of mature concentration.

'Even when they share the same bed?' he enquired mildly.

For a few seconds she had to think about that one, then her face cleared. 'Watching television in the same room. Your brother and I aren't *sleeping together*, and you have a sordid mind if you can't believe that.'

'I prefer to call it *experienced*.'

'Then I guess that we just agree to differ.' She shrugged, tugging back the reins on her imagination, which threatened to veer off down those *experienced* paths to which he had alluded. Oh, yes, she had heard all about Curtis Greene's experience. There had never been a time, she had been told by Andy one evening, when the drink had overcome his natural reserve about his brother, when Curtis had not had an adoring female at his side. For *experienced male* she preferred to read *practised womaniser*.

'So,' she asked into the growing silence between them, 'how long do you plan on staying in London?' A particularly tactless question, she realised, as soon as she had uttered it.

'Long enough to have a word with my brother.' He stretched out his long legs in front of him and crossed them lightly at the ankles. 'A very serious word.'

Jade licked her lips nervously and felt a protective rush of feeling. This visit was going to shock Andy to the core. He wasn't ready to deal with Curtis and all the demons associated with him. Not yet.

'I don't suppose you'll listen to a word I tell you, but can I ask you not to be hard on Andy?'

For some reason he seemed to find the request amusing.

'Not be hard on Andy? Since you two seem to be so touchingly close, you must know that I've been in charge of his welfare from the time he was eight years old and I was an old man of twenty-one?'

His eyes darkened and she caught something in there, the shadow of regret, but the moment was fleeting enough to make her doubt what she had seen. He leaned forward, his body rigid, and hit one open palm forcefully with his closed fist. The subdued violence behind the gesture made her wince. It also made her determined to fight this man all the way, if only to protect his brother.

'Being hard was the only way to teach Andy how to cope with his wealth, how to cope with *life*. In case you hadn't noticed, it's a bloody tough world out there, and when our parents died, it fell to me to teach him how to cope with it.' His eyes glittered.

'Well, he's not a child of eight any longer,' Jade said

steadily, 'and maybe he's learnt whatever lessons he needed to learn to give him the strength to go his own way.'

'Is that the sort of claptrap psychobabble you've been pouring into his head? As one good friend to another? Feeding him with idiotic notions about running away from the rat race and *doing his own thing* with bits of clay and oil paint?' He laughed acidly. 'You must have thought you'd hit jackpot in my brother.'

'I told you, I'm not interested in Andy for his money.' She heard the trace of contempt in her voice, and knew that he had caught it as well, from his sudden stillness. 'And I haven't *fed* him with any notions of doing anything. In case you hadn't noticed, he's got a mind of his own!'

'And he's suddenly decided to veer away from his very lucrative job running the family business so that he can become a hack painter. All without any persuasive support from you, his very good and very *platonic* friend. Now, why do I find that so hard to believe?'

'Because you have a suspicious nature?'

'And, by some stunning coincidence, you too were going through the same agonies of indecision, so you decided to throw in your very good job, whatever that may be, to pursue the same ridiculous career calling. What *was* your job, as a matter of interest?'

She debated whether to tell him or not, and quickly came to the conclusion that the more open she was in certain areas, the sooner she would get him off her back.

'I worked for a small computer firm,' she said shortly. 'I was personal assistant to the director there, but really I ran the place and was financially rewarded for it.'

'Then why leave?'

'Because...because I wanted a change of scenery.'

He shook his head in a gesture of irritated frustration. 'From highly paid personal assistant to dabbling with crayons. That's quite a change, Miss Summers. So you and Andy do what, exactly…? Sit around in the evenings, playing at being artists, which is really just another way of saying avoiding responsibility and kidding yourselves that the real world doesn't exist because you've chosen to retreat from it? Or is it all just some elaborate courtship? Are you just biding your time over the coloured pencils, eyeing him hungrily, waiting to see when would be the best time to slip under the covers with him?'

Jade gave up. Curtis Greene, finding himself confronted with a situation over which he had almost no control, was responding in probably the only way he knew how. By a process of intimidation and cunning. Every word she said and every truth she uttered would be twisted into something sinister and riddled with insinuation.

She sighed and silently reflected on the future hassle of trying to find somewhere to rent.

'Yes. You're right. I'm a vicious, heartless gold-digger who engineered your brother into taking an interest in painting, and to further the illusion of comradeship I decided to toss my own very good job aside so that I could sit around drawing and pretending to be an artist. And, yes, it's all an elaborate ploy because at night, over the coloured pencils, I'm really carving out a future where I become mistress of the big house and queen of the castle.

'You've caught me napping, as a matter of fact. Normally I'm not dressed in an old pair of jeans and a tee shirt. Oh, no, normally I'm decked out in all my finery on the off chance that my victim might just stroll unexpectedly through the front door. Daylight never sees me without my silver or gold high-heeled shoes, my hair perfectly coiffeured, my nails painted scarlet and an interesting and revealing dress of Lycra. There. Satisfied?'

She looked at him and was invigorated to see him temporarily stumped. He hadn't expected that response out of her. He had geared himself up for an exhaustive chipping away at all her defences until he was satisfied.

'That's a very childish response, Miss Summers,' he said eventually, and she would have given herself a hearty pat on the back for having won this round of the battle if it hadn't been for the glint lurking in the depths of his ice-blue eyes.

'I'm just telling you what you want to hear. You're determined not to believe a word I say to you so what's the use my trying?'

'Course,' he said thoughtfully, 'who am I to disbelieve you when you say that you swan about wearing tight dresses and high heels?' He gave her a slow, thorough and leisurely inspection. 'I imagine you would look very...what's the word I'm looking for, here?...alluring?...appealing? Or maybe just...sexy...in a tight Lycra dress with high gold shoes. That translucent, mobile face, just the right interesting mixture of innocence and experience, those eyes with just the right hint of sadness...yes, in a small outfit it would be quite stunning, I imagine...and I can't get much of an idea about your body, but from what I can see...'

'That's enough!' Her skin seemed to have erupted into tingling goosebumps and she was leaning forward in her chair, clutching it, in fact, her face flushed.

'Oh, I'm sorry. Am I embarrassing you?' He smiled very slowly at her, which sent her self-control plummeting a few more notches. He waited for a while, watching her as she tried to mobilise her brain into action, then rescued her from the situation by asking what time his brother would be home.

'Later this afternoon,' Jade said, licking her lips. 'He has a lecture at two-thirty and then he usually goes to the library for an hour or so afterwards. I think he was supposed to be meeting a few friends later on, but I don't know whether he will or not. He said that he just wanted to come home and flop in front of the television with a Chinese takeaway. Normally, I cook something, well, we take it in turns, but he's a much better cook than I am. In fact, he's brilliant. I don't suppose you know that.'

She was rattling. On and on and on to cover the sudden and overwhelming confusion generated by his casual, stray observations about her. The man had a golden tongue, or at least gilt-edged, and he had chosen to wield it on her, and it had had the desired effect, throwing her into a tizzy.

And he talked about *her* being manipulative! How many women had he lured into his bed using that same, knowing charm? Whatever he had wanted to know about her relationship with Andy, she had somehow satisfied him. His posture indicated as much. He was more relaxed. Gearing up to round two, she thought despondently. Her appearance when he had not been expecting it had doubtless taken him by surprise, but he had not been so flabbergasted that he hadn't used the situation to his advantage, and for the moment he was content that she was above board. She could be dispatched without further ado. Time to get himself ready for the next phase, which would doubtless be working on his brother, trying to persuade him back into DGG Holdings, the prestigious company that seemed to own everything under the sun under some umbrella or other.

'Cookery? No. I can't say I was aware of Andy's talents in that direction, but then he's never had much of an opportunity to practise them on me. I've been out of the country for the past few years.' He glanced at his watch, and she could see him working out in his head whether it was worth his while remaining here or leaving to return later.

She was no longer of consequence. She had been dealt with.

'Yes, I know. Look, there's no need for you to stay here. I don't know when exactly Andy will be home...'

'I'll have a quick look around the old place,' he said smoothly, standing up. 'Care to come along?'

Jade sprang to her feet as well and heaved a sigh of relief. 'No! Take your time. I have loads of work to carry on doing, so if you don't mind...'

'Sure,' he said genially, moving towards her. 'Forget I'm here. I know how you artists like peace to work in, and I wouldn't want to get in the line of any artistic temperament.'

'I don't possess any such thing.' Jade stayed her ground, out of politeness and a desire to prove to herself that she could remain unruffled by this man.

'No?' He looked at her sideways and she was uncomfortably aware that from where he was standing she had done nothing *but* react with artistic temperament, from the minute she had laid eyes on him. Pointless to try and explain that she was normally as calm as a lake and that all that brimstone and fire was not part and parcel of her emotional make up. He had simply managed to bring out the worst in her.

'Absolutely not. None at all. I rarely raise my voice, in fact. I'm a very calm person.' He continued to look at her with amused disbelief and she could feel a lot of that so-called calm ebbing out of her.

'Maybe it's just me, then,' he told her piously, and she glared at him from under dark eyebrows.

'Yes, it *is* just you, actually!' she snapped. 'What do you expect? You show up here out of the blue and proceed to subject me to a tirade of unfounded accusations!' She could hear her voice spiralling higher and she took a deep, steadying breath.

The man was insufferable.

And why was he just standing there with that stupid grin on his face, as though he was the cat that had managed to corner the bowl of cream?

'You don't know how relieved I am to hear you say that.'

'What? What are you talking about *now*?' She was finding it difficult to keep up with his rapid shifts in mood. It was like being on a rollercoaster. No wonder he was such a big name in business. He probably addled his competitors to death!

'Well, I might have to readjust my ideas if I thought that you were acting out of character simply because of my personality...'

'I have no idea what you're on about.' She began walking out of the door, aware of him a few paces behind her.

'I mean,' he said to her back, 'if I addled you, then I might jump to the conclusion that it was because I turned you on. Sexual electricity manifests itself in myriad ways, you know.'

That had her spinning back on her heels to confront him, her body arched forward belligerently.

'You? *Turn me on*? Ha! In case no one's ever mentioned it before, *you* are the most infuriating human on the face of this planet! Not to mention the most egotistical!'

'So I can look forward to a calm little stay here, then, with no jealous sibling rivalry?'

She was still fuming over his arrogance and it took her a few seconds to absorb what he had said. When she did, her eyes opened wider in horrified disbelief.

'Calm little *stay here*?' she asked, bewildered. 'What do you mean by *little stay*?'

'Well, Miss Summers, you can't expect me to rush back

to New York when I have to step into my brother's shoes now that he's left his job to become an artist, can you?' He shrugged and gave her a long-suffering look which did not meld well with the aggressive lines of his face. Humility, she thought sourly, was an emotion he only occasionally flirted with. If that. 'Unless I can persuade him to knock all these stupid daydreams of becoming another Matisse on the head...' He paused to allow his words to sink in, in all their sickening detail. 'And, however much I want to give you the benefit of the doubt, I *know* you'll appreciate that I might want to linger on here, keep an eye on the situation until I'm fully satisfied that you are what you say you are.' The blue eyes were rueful, but underneath the phoney expression of regret she could see the hardness all too clearly.

'So you'll be hanging around,' she said dully.

'That's right! Might be just for a few days...might be a few weeks...who knows? Might even be for longer...I'm a man who likes to go with the flow, so to speak.' He eyed the staircase, then her. 'Hence my desire to become reacquainted with my house. See where I'm going to sleep.' He flashed her a broad, dazzling smile. 'Have fun drawing!'

He headed up the stairs, his long legs covering ground rapidly until he was out of sight, while Jade remained where she was, dumbstruck, and wondering how the day had ended on such an awful note.

When the doorbell rang, she answered it with the resignation of someone expecting the worst.

'Morning, love.' The man was short, ruddy complexioned and dressed in overalls with an off-colour bomber jacket. He consulted the piece of paper in his hand. 'Got the right 'ouse, 'ave I? I'm the plumber, 'ere about a leak.'

CHAPTER THREE

IT WAS a little after nine in the evening when Jade quietly opened the front door, risked a nervous glance at the hallway and the staircase winding temptingly up to her bedroom. With a little sigh of relief, she closed the door very silently behind her, standing still as it clunked firmly shut. Just in case. Just in case Curtis came bounding out from behind a door somewhere like a bloodhound on the scent of something tasty and her peace of mind was shattered. Yet again. For the sixth day running.

If she had hoped that his appearance at Stratton House might have caused a few ripples before ebbing away into a relative state of calm, then it was becoming increasingly clear that this was not to be the case.

'This is ridiculous,' Andy had complained the day before, over a cup of coffee in one of the college canteens. She had watched the droop of his mouth as he listlessly stirred his coffee with concern. 'He's been working all the hours God made from as far back as I can remember. Yet he now chooses to saunter back home at seven in the evening so that we can all sit down to a cosy little family meal. What a joke!'

It didn't take a genius to figure out his tactics, Jade had thought sourly. Curtis Greene, empire-builder and workaholic, was trooping home so that he could keep an eye on them, not that dear Andy suspected a thing. She hadn't mentioned any of his brother's grim accusations and she had no intention of doing so. As far as she was concerned, the boat had been rocked enough already, without her adding to the general seasickness.

'Maybe he's trying to bond,' she'd suggested, and they had looked at one another with glum, resigned understanding.

'Bond, flond. All I've had off him are lectures on responsibility and growing up. I'm twenty-two years old!' He'd raised aquamarine eyes to hers and grimaced. 'He just can't seem to get it through that thick skull of his that I'm determined to pursue my art!'

'Well, you'll just have to prove to him that you mean business,' she had said gently.

Easier said than done, she thought now. The only business Curtis understood was the complex business of making money, and after his initial flaming row with Andy he had subsided into the age-old water-dripping-on-stone routine. Over drinks, he would sit, cradling his gin and tonic with a vaguely glowering expression, and refer to the importance of keeping their vast business under family control.

Over dinner, he would punctuate the stilted conversation with observations on the harshness of life and the necessity of confronting it and controlling it, by which he meant packing in thoughts of painting and doing what his family legacy dictated, and over coffee he would throw dark hints about hangers-on, apparently rife in the world of art, who would see the heir to a fortune as easy game. These remarks were the ones that Jade found most difficult to deal with, because she knew that they referred to her but were never couched in terms that would allow her a say on the matter. Not without stirring up a hornets' nest.

So far Andy had stuck his ground, but for how much longer? Curtis was forceful, and determined to have his way, and she knew that he was just biding his time, confident that he would get precisely what he wanted in the end.

They could leave the place, and in fact they had discussed this option, but, as Andy had said, that would be tantamount to running away, and he had spent his life running away. And Jade, he had informed her desperately, couldn't leave him alone with Curtis. She was his moral support, and he needed her.

So here they were, the three of them, stuck in the rambling house, with the Master Puppeteer waiting for his chance to pull some strings.

She was tiptoeing up the stairs, gaining confidence that she would make it to bed without obstruction, when, from the foot of the staircase, she heard that dark, velvety voice call out.

'You're back. I've been waiting to have a word with you.'

She spun around guiltily and remained in frozen animation, with one hand on the banister, the other clutching the lapels of her jacket.

'I'm kind of tired. Can it wait?'

'I'm in the blue sitting room.'

So much for deigning to answer her question. She watched, in frustration, his vanishing back, and then reluctantly made her way back down the stairs and towards the sitting room, divesting herself of her jacket *en route*.

She really *was* tired. Andy was not back home this evening, and in an attempt to defer her own moment of return she had slugged it out at college, gone to the library and then forced herself to go for drinks with a group of students whose high spirits had only made her feel old and washed out. It was bad enough that she sported none of the prerequisites of the struggling art student. Her hair was its natural colour, her make-up was subdued, her clothes made no statement whatsoever unless you called *feeling comfortable* a statement, and getting drunk on a regular basis was something she viewed with horror rather than delight.

She walked into the sitting room to find Curtis standing by the bay window with a glass in one hand.

'I've poured you a drink.' He nodded to the glass on the table in the centre of the room. 'Take it. Might relax you. You act as though I'm about to eat you the minute you're within five feet of me.'

Jade snatched up the drink and swallowed a couple of large mouthfuls, then sat down rapidly as the burning liquid shot through her system like fire.

'What did you want to talk to me about?'

'Where's my brother?'

'Isn't he at home?' she asked innocently, wishing that he would do the polite thing and sit down, because he looked even more forbidding standing by the bay window, his body thrown into irregular shadows.

'No, and you know it. Isn't that why you made sure to stay out of the house for as long as possible?' He looked at his watch and gave a theatrically overdone frown of perplexity. 'If this is the latest you can do, then your social life could do with an injection. Where is he, anyway? I wanted to discuss some business with him.'

Jade looked at him with annoyance. Typically, he had shoved one provocative remark down her throat then moved onto something else so smoothly that she was left with only the sour aftertaste of his comment.

'I don't *know* where he is. He's a young boy. I suspect he's somewhere with his friends, having a wild time.'

'He's a *young boy*? You sound as though you're a hundred and one!' He flashed her a dazzling smile that only made her feel even more ruffled, and threw his head back so that he could finish the contents of his glass in one gulp.

He had obviously returned from work some time earlier, because he was no longer in his suit, but wearing a pair of casual black cords and a long-sleeved black jumper, the sleeves of which he had shoved up to his elbows. The whole outfit gave him the air of a bandit. All that was missing was the scar on the face, something which, she thought, sipping her drink, she could help out with.

'I'm surprised you let him out for the night.' He paused suggestively in mid-stride as he poured himself another drink from the ornamental wooden bar in the corner of the room. 'Very trusting of you. But then I can tell from what I've seen that you two seem to have a very trusting relationship with one another.' He swirled his glass around gently. 'Not a good idea, you know. Out of sight, out of mind, I believe the saying goes.'

'Did you ask me to come in here so that you could dazzle me with your knowledge of proverbs?'

This time his grin was more expansive, but no less unsettling. He was absolutely right when he said that as soon as she came within five feet of him her nervous system started developing a will of its own. In an effort to counteract the symptom she finished her drink and then leaned forward, legs crossed, hands nervously clasped on one knee.

'Aren't you afraid that my dear brother might be unwinding with a less challenging bimbo in a bed somewhere?'

'No, actually.' She smiled secretly, unaware that the smile altered her face completely, turned her blonde attractiveness into something wicked and sexy.

'You should have informed me that neither of you would be returning to eat dinner. I would have let Annie have the evening off.' His voice was clipped, and he pushed himself away from the bay window and sat down in one of the chairs.

Annie had been his glorious idea as soon as he'd moved back. She was one of the company caterers and he had decided, against their protests, to employ her as a cook.

'We don't *have* to inform you of our whereabouts!' Jade snapped. 'We were perfectly happy...'

'Just *being*. Until the big, bad wolf came along with other ideas. Yes, yes, yes. I've heard variations on the theme before.'

'Why are you so obsessed with having control over everybody's lives?'

'Care for another drink?'

'No. I'm not accustomed...' There he went again, veering away from the topic and denying her the opportunity to let rip. Her counsellor would have a field-day, she thought. From anxious and repressed to wanting to let rip the minute Curtis Greene so much as glanced in her direction.

'What a good little girl you are. I'm beginning to revise all my opinions,' he said thoughtfully. 'Perhaps you're *not* the malign influence I first thought. Perhaps you're the best thing that ever happened to my brother.'

Why didn't she believe him?

'Course, I *could* be wrong...'

'You? Wrong?' She looked at him with exaggerated incredulity. 'Surely not!'

'It's been known to happen, though not very often.'

'Naturally not.'

'For instance, I was way off target when I assumed that my brother would take over the running of the company and stick it out...'

'He did it for a year and a half...' She knew that he had

started his art course after leaving school, only to buckle under pressure and capitulate into working in an office.

'Not exactly a long time in the scheme of things, though, was it?'

Long enough to know that it wasn't what he wanted to do, she thought. It was only when they had become firm friends that he had confided in her the depth of his unhappiness and frustration. Getting dressed in his suit and going into the company had been, for him, his definition of hell.

'What's his future as an artist?' Curtis asked, losing his temper. 'I mean, let's be honest here, *where exactly* is all that rubbish going to get him? He qualifies in art, and then what? Runs around living off his trust fund? *What?*' He raked his long fingers through his hair in exasperated frustration and stood up, pacing the room as though movement was the only way to release some of the energy coursing through him.

'Well?' he demanded, stopping in front of her and staring down into her face. Jade, obliged to look back up at him, pressed herself further back into the chair. '*You* tell *me!*' he bit out. 'You're in the same boat! What's going through your heads?' As though not content with his bullet-style line of delivery, guaranteed to stifle the power of speech in all but the most hardened, he proceeded to lean over her, supporting himself with his hands on either side of her chair, and in the process sending all coherent thought to the four winds.

Now, not only was she forced to stare into his eyes, she could also feel his warm breath against her face. In some strange way it acted like a fan on a budding fire, sending her pulses racing.

'It's all about finding yourself,' she protested weakly. 'I mean, I don't know what Andy—'

'Yes, you damn well do! Don't think I haven't noticed

how you two interact with one another! The way you glance at one another as though you can communicate without speaking!'

She was finding it hard to comprehend the exact meaning of his words. She was too busy trying to fight off the effect he was having on her.

'He just wants to live his own life!' she blurted out, and was rewarded with a perplexed shake of the head.

'Of course he wants to live his own bloody life! I'm not trying to stop him!'

'Yes, you are! You came over here to try and force him back into the company and you haven't let up! You're not interested in what your brother does, just as long as it's a course of action you approve of! Namely, going back out to work for the family firm!'

This time he flushed darkly and pushed himself away from her. Very slowly, she felt her breathing return to normal.

'So what do you suggest I do? Vanish and let him proceed to ruin his life?'

'He won't be *ruining his life*. How dramatic can you get? And even if he *does* end up ruining his life, as you put it, then, yes! Let him!'

'God, this is a nightmare.' He sat back down and rested his head back against the chair, closing his eyes and letting all the anger drain away from his face. Without it, his latent sexuality became almost overwhelming. She found herself staring at him, fascinated, and had to make an effort to look away or risk being caught red-handed.

'I couldn't believe it when I got that faxed letter of resignation. At first I thought it was some kind of joke. Fair enough for Sarah to take herself off to Australia on some journey of self-discovery, but Andy! The helm was ready and waiting for him.' Underneath the fury and bluster, she felt a sharp twinge of sympathy. However misguided his actions, his intentions were honourable. He was simply looking out for his brother, and this was the only way he knew how.

Funny, but she had spent the past couple of years so wrapped up in her own problems, her own unique situation, that she had removed herself emotionally from the rest of the human race. She interacted with them, but only superficially. Deep inside, she held herself apart, and now she could feel herself opening back up to other people, becoming involved with their problems and motivations.

And at the centre of it, like the eye of the hurricane, was Curtis Greene.

'He won't change his mind,' she said eventually. 'And it's unfair of you to try and whip him into submission.'

'That's a bit of an exaggeration, isn't it?' He opened his eyes to look at her drily.

'If you'd heard yourself, you wouldn't say that.' There were a few seconds' silence, during which she gradually realised that the atmosphere between them had altered. She laughed nervously.

'Is that it, then?'

'Is what it?' In time, she thought, she might learn to ignore his questions, because as soon as she asked for clarification she knew that clarification was going to be the last thing she wanted.

He continued to look at her with lazy interest, and whatever fury had been raging through him moments before now seemed to have disappeared completely, or else had been thoroughly shut away to be extracted, alive and kicking, at some later date. For the while, his interest was focused on her and her entirely. The completeness of his scrutiny made her flush.

'Your relationship with my brother. Is it more of a maternal thing? He lost his mother when he was a child. Maybe—who knows?—he sees you as a sort of mother substitute.'

'I hadn't really thought about it from that angle,' Jade confessed awkwardly.

'Yes, that could be it, I suppose. A mother figure. In the intellectual sense of the word.' His eyes flicked over her and he smiled with indolent charm. 'Definitely not in the literal sense. Which, of course, begs the obvious question...'

'Which is?' There I go again, she thought, falling into the trap once more.

'What do *you* see in him? Does the *little boy lost* scenario turn you on? Do you get off on feeling that someone else is emotionally dependent on you? Is it your kind of aphrodisiac?' He laughed under his breath at her expression of outrage and then, true to form, carried on speaking, so that she couldn't jump in with an appropriately heated response. 'Well, that's by the by. Still leaves me with a lot of questions about *you*, though... Here you are, you've given up your job...you know, sometimes when people adopt a complete change of lifestyle it says a great deal about them...'

'Who's into the psychobabble now?' Jade asked feebly. He was getting nearer. With every passing moment she could feel him circling her, getting closer and closer to the core of her, and more than anything else she didn't want him there. He wasn't the kind of man she had ever been attracted to and she had seen from close up how untrustworthy men like him could be. Caroline had always surrounded herself with charmers who had invariably turned out to be cads. No, she, Jade, went for the kind, stolid type, and she was mystified by her own response to Curtis. After being numb for so many years she couldn't understand why *he* had to be the one around when life was slowly seeping back into her.

'Sometimes,' he drawled thoughtfully, 'people will change every aspect of their lives in an attempt to run away from something...is that your problem? Are you running away from something? *Or someone?* You're twenty-six years old but you obviously don't have a rampant social life...'

'By which I take it you mean that I don't change my bed partners with the same regularity as I change my bed linen...?'

'...and something's driven you to jack in your job to study... What? What drove you to do that? And why did you go peculiar that first evening when I said something...what was it? Do you remember? I made some passing remark and you looked as though you were suddenly going to pass out... Whatever's going on here, it's not all that it seems, is it?' He touched two fingers together and tapped them lightly on his chin. 'It's all a bit of a mystery, and would you just believe it? I love mysteries. I love unravelling them. I find it very satisfying.'

'Is—is that so?' Jade stammered.

'It certainly is.' He narrowed his eyes and looked at her with speculation. 'Such a challenge. *Sensing* that there's something beneath the surface and then digging away until I get to what it is.' He expelled his breath and resumed his musing, unnerving monologue. 'In this particular jigsaw puzzle I get the impression that there are quite a few missing pieces, and you can rest assured that I intend to get to them.'

'Why?' She shook her head dumbly. 'Not that there's anything to find out,' she added belatedly.

'Why? Good question. Primarily it's to do with my brother's welfare. I don't know *where* the hell you've sprung out of, and I haven't heard any nightly goings on down the corridor between rooms, but it'd be nice to make sure that you haven't got some kind of sinister hidden agenda. You don't *look* it, I have to tell you, but then looks can be so deceiving, can't they? Pays not to trust people on appearances. And then, let's just say that I'm *curious*. You can understand that, can't you?'

'For someone who's so hot on proverbs, you should know the one about curiosity and the cat.'

'Ah, yes, but I've always thought that that cat must have been particularly stupid. Not one of my sins, you'll be impressed to hear. Where were you living before you moved here?'

'Hampstead,' Jade told him warily.

'Nice. So, you've lived in London all your life, have you?'

'No.'

'How long have you been here?'

She looked at him, not too sure how to proceed, but since none of this information came under the category of trade secrets, she said, with hesitation, 'A little over two years.'

'And before that?'

'Near Stratford. There. Satisfied? Can I go now?'

'How could I stop you?' He shrugged eloquently. 'You're a free agent. Course you can go. Although I must admit that I'm beginning to enjoy our little conversation.'

'That's because you're a sadist.'

She hadn't expected him to find that as funny as he did. He burst out laughing, and after a while she found herself grudgingly smiling because his laughter was so infectious. Their eyes tangled, and she looked away hurriedly.

'You should just try giving Andy a chance,' she rushed on, aware of some inexplicable churning inside her. 'I can understand that you don't sympathise with his decision to leave the family business, and I know that that must be a bit inconvenient for you, but it would mean so much to him if you would just take a bit of an interest in what he's doing. You haven't asked him once what his course involves. It's as though you want to pretend that it doesn't exist.

'There's going to be an exhibition of some of the course work for we first-year students in a week's time. You should come along. It's so narrow-minded to write it all off as a waste of time without even bothering to see any of it.'

He didn't look as though he was about to say anything in response to her. He was quite happy to watch her and listen to her witter herself into silence.

'How is it that you don't mind Andy doing his own thing without you? If there's nothing sexual between you, then is it because you have a man of your own? I haven't seen any sight of him. You ought to bring him here, introduce him to the family. Or is he hidden away somewhere in the background, like a leper?'

'Are you listening to a word I'm telling you?' She stood up, frustrated and embarrassed, and he followed suit, to her dismay walking over slowly to where she was standing, his blue eyes curious and amused.

'Course—I've listened to every word you've just said.' He looked down at her, his hands casually shoved into his pockets. 'Avidly. And I have to confess that you do have a point. Perhaps I *will* take more of an interest in Andy's course.' He smiled disarmingly at her. 'You know what they say, if you can't beat 'em, join 'em. Oops, another proverb. At this rate you're going to categorise me as a crashing bore as well as a narrow-minded tyrant. No, I simply decided to change the subject because the prospect of finding out a bit more about my unexpected tenant was too tantalising to resist. So *is* there a mysterious lover waiting in the wings? You might as well answer me, you know. That way you won't end up having to dodge my questions.'

'No, there's no lover waiting in the wings.' She sighed deeply and pointedly and with resounding boredom.

'No? Correct me if I'm wrong, but if there's no sex in your life, then my sensitive antennae are telling me that you're either resting or else you're recovering from a broken relationship.'

'Yes, well, *my* sensitive antennae are telling me that it's time for sleep.'

What, she wondered, was the description of someone who was beyond infuriating and relentless? Whatever it was, Curtis Greene headed the list.

'No, it's not,' he denied on a murmur, 'it's telling you that it's time to run away from me. You're not *scared* of me, are you, Jade?'

'No, I am *not* scared of you!' she cried feverishly. 'I think that you're a...a nuisance!'

'Ouch. That hurts.' But he was still smiling, and his smile was like a drug, if there was such a drug that might turn someone's brain to cotton wool and paralyse their vocal cords. 'Well, maybe you're scared of what I may find out *about* you.'

There he went again, searching and rooting around, trying to piece her together, looking for answers.

'You can stop worrying,' he said softly, leaning forward so that he was almost touching her. 'I've watched you and my brother over the past week and I have a gut feeling that you were telling the truth. There's no electricity between the two of you. Don't misunderstand me. There's *something* between the two of you, but it's not passion.'

'I guess that means that you'll be heading back to New York pretty soon...?'

'And leave behind my unfinished jigsaw puzzle?' He

clicked his tongue in a reproving manner. 'Besides, there's a lot of work to be done on the business here, and I have to say that, having stayed out of London for such a long time, I'm finding that it holds certain attractions that The Big Apple doesn't. There's more room to breathe over here. I'd go so far as to say that I'm rather enjoying myself. And you're so close to Andy, I'm sure you'd be delighted if we got a little closer to one another.' He paused and raised one eyebrow enquiringly. 'Build a few bridges, so to speak.'

'And you never thought of building these bridges before now?'

He flushed, and then moved away slightly, propping himself up against the doorframe.

'I...it was not a straightforward situation,' he said roughly.

'Situations are as straightforward as you make them,' Jade responded, more confident now that they were not discussing *her*, nor was he standing inches away. At least she could breathe properly. 'No,' she amended, thinking of her own convoluted scenario with a piercing sense of regret. 'No, perhaps that's not quite true.' Her eyes clouded over, but before she could give him time to jump in with his usual battery of interested questions she continued in a stern voice, 'But I can't see *what* prevented you from getting to know Andy. He's your brother!' At least you're not alone in the world, she nearly added.

'He was a child when I took over the running of the company! What can you expect? I never had the *time* to get to know him. I was too busy running a company and looking after his educational needs! And his sister's!' He shook his head and looked at her with accusation, as though she had somehow manoeuvred him into this position when he hadn't been expecting it. 'Then things started to go pear-shaped in our New York branch. Fraud, embezzlement, you name it. I had to get out there, fast, and by the time it got sorted out the years had rolled by.'

'What were you doing *before*…your parents died?' Jade asked curiously, and was surprised to see that the look he gave her was almost sheepish.

'Getting used to not studying,' he said, shrugging. 'I'd done the university bit and was in the process of bumming around, taking time out for a few months before I got my teeth into taking over the business.'

'*You* were *bumming around*?'

'Yes, well, it's not that inconceivable,' he said with a certain amount of annoyed defiance. 'Believe it or not, I wasn't *born* wearing a suit and carrying a briefcase.'

'But you always knew that you would wind up taking over the running of your father's company?'

'Nosy little thing when you get going, aren't you?'

'Makes a change,' she muttered by way of response, and he grinned at her.

'No, I didn't know from the age of five that I was destined to head the family firm, but, yes, I can't say I'm shocked and appalled to find myself in the place where I am now.'

'But didn't you ever want to…stretch your wings? Do something different?'

'You mean like live in a commune, or write poetry, or take up transcendental meditation?'

'All those things, yes,' Jade said gravely, and this time when he laughed she found herself laughing back.

'You should be thanking me…again,' he murmured huskily, his eyes not leaving her face. They were not always the colour of winter sea, she thought distractedly. Their colour shifted and changed according to his mood. Right now they were a deep, true blue, more the shade of Andy's but without the transparency.

'For what?'

'For making you laugh.' He looked at her seriously and gently. 'Why have you found laughter difficult...?'

She felt the breath catch in her throat. She knew, from what her counsellor had said, that she had to relinquish her need to keep her emotions to herself, nurturing them like hothouse plants, carefully tending them even while she felt the sharp prickles on their stems cutting into her skin. But it had never been in her nature to pour her soul out to anyone, and ever since Caroline had died she had dried up completely. She stared at him mutely, then finally hung her head, biting down the urge to cry.

'Is this to do with another man? Because if it is, your energy is misspent. Speaking as one of the species, I can tell you that they are very rarely worth the tide of emotion that can linger on after a relationship goes sour.'

'No,' she whispered. 'It's nothing to do with a man.' She wiped an errant tear from the corner of her eye. 'I must go. I'm very tired.'

She stepped towards him and he reached out, blocking her path out with his hand, which lay flat-fisted against the opposite doorframe. With his other hand, he tilted her face up to his.

'I haven't made things very easy for you here. If you're going through a rough time and I've added to it, then please accept my apologies.'

She couldn't deny that he was being utterly sincere. He would rant and rail at Andy's decision, and at the mess he seemed to think would dog his brother's footsteps, but she knew that if he were to be proved wrong then he would be humble in defeat. She smiled wanly and grimaced.

'I understand; I really do. It's just that...'

'That what...?'

'Things are never as simple as they seem,' was all she could find to say.

'Some things are.'

She hadn't been expecting it, so when his mouth covered hers, her initial reaction was not to pull away. He cupped the small of her back and pulled her towards him, and the small fire which had been burning ever since she'd seen him standing on the doorstep turned into a conflagration. She gave a small, surprised, helpless moan and kissed him back, releasing passions she had never suspected were there. She felt as if she was being engulfed in wetness. The wetness of their mouths greedily uniting. The wetness that was telling her how much of her womanhood she had put into hibernation.

It felt like hours but it must have only been a matter of a minute, then she was pushing against him, struggling and half sobbing.

She wouldn't, *couldn't*, let herself capitulate. Not to him, not to anyone. The thought of it alone felt like treachery.

'Let me go!' But in fact he had already let her go. She waited until some of her calm was restored, breathing deeply, not daring to look at him, because that would have just made her mortification complete.

She forced a brave, brittle smile onto her lips, looked past his left shoulder, which was not nearly enough to deflect the intensity of his gaze on her, nodded as though vaguely agreeing with something that had been said, and then fled.

CHAPTER FOUR

JADE had decided from the start that she would avoid her own work, eight detailed illustrations which had impressed her tutor, until the last possible moment. It was the first time she had taken part in an amateur exhibition of such size. She had been expecting a much smaller and much more modest display of the course work, and she and Andy had strolled into the college to find themselves in the midst of a proper exhibition. The bright, airy rooms, with their white, clinical walls, were teeming with people. Students, friends and relatives of students, and the rumour was flying around, art connoisseurs, who were testing the ground, sizing up the talent for future reference.

When this rumour had reached their ears she and Andy had both covertly looked around, but there were a lot of men in suits and women nodding knowledgeably, and they had both admitted, giggling nervously, that they probably wouldn't recognise an art connoisseur from a double glazing salesman.

The paintings and sculptures had been grouped according to styles, and it was clear that a considerable amount of time had been taken arranging the displays. From where she was standing now, in a group of strangers, all of whom looked like possible art connoisseurs, she could glimpse Sean MacFarley's large, dramatic oil canvasses—abstract commentaries on industrial life in the North. Someone was pointing to the details of the line work and she clutched Andy's hand with sudden, anxious panic.

'I can't go near my stuff,' she whispered gloomily, tugging him away. 'I can just imagine all these people standing in front of my minuscule illustrations snorting with laughter.'

'Big isn't *always* beautiful,' Andy whispered back soothingly. 'Trust me on that, darling.'

'At least you *look* like an artist.'

'Do you mean impoverished and bedraggled?'

'I mean,' she said drily, 'Adonis-like and individualistic.' He did too. He was wearing a pair of black bell-bottomed trousers and an eye-catching silk shirt with strange swirly designs which he had hanging loose, and he had swept his blond hair to the back in a small ponytail. He looked beautiful and stylish.

'You have your own look too,' he said, eyeing her dubiously, and she grinned at him.

'Yes. The *shouldn't-I-be-at-a-business-school?* look.'

'Stop crying yourself down.'

'Sorry.' She giggled. 'You're right.' Someone swept past with a tray of white wine and she reached out and helped herself to a glass, which she swigged down in two gulps. The restorative powers of alcohol, she thought. She could now face the prospect of viewing her own work without fearing the mental scenario which involved ten would-be art connoisseurs, guffaws of laughter and cries of *Rubbish!* A few more glasses and she might even find that she no longer cared one way or another who sniggered at her work.

They spent a few minutes chatting to some of their tutors, then meandered in the general direction of 'Landscape', and as Jade idly looked around her, the smile on her mouth froze.

'Don't look around now, Andy,' she muttered, tugging him down to her level, 'but we have an unexpected guest.'

Even in this crowd, Curtis stood out like a sore thumb. He was suit-clad, like quite a number of the men, but even in the uniform of pinstripe charcoal-grey, he still managed to grab the eye and hold it. In fact, she noticed that quite a number of people, particularly those of the female variety, were staring at him covertly. The term 'Art in Motion' came to her mind, and she concealed a sudden urge to burst out laughing. Physically, he fitted the description like a glove, but spiritually she figured she would be hard placed to find someone less in line with the description than Curtis Greene.

'I'm not looking,' Andy muttered back with a theatrically conspiratorial facial expression. 'But does she look like someone who would be interested in becoming my patron?'

'It's a *he*.'

'He, she, *it*...would I have seen his face on the cover of an important arts magazine, clutching his wallet and bellowing that he needed to find good young talent to fling his money at...?'

'You don't *need* the money,' Jade pointed out, watching as Curtis moved through the crowd, pausing to glance without expression at the various pieces hanging on the walls. He looked neither impressed nor disgusted. As usual, his face gave nothing away. A tall red-haired woman came to stand alongside him, and Jade could see them conversing politely about Robert Rendall's controversial piece of sculpture which was meant to depict *Man Holding World*, but looked to her very much like a large blob of clay which had been tinkered about with by a ten-year-old child and then left to gather cobwebs.

'I do,' Andy was informing her in a pained voice. 'For my sense of self-worth.' He angled his body slightly, followed the direction of her gaze and then released a strangled gasp. 'God, what's *he* doing here?'

'Sudden interest in the world of art?' she suggested. Right now, if someone came past with another tray of wine, she thought, she would just keep the entire tray to herself and down the contents of what was on it.

'Don't make me laugh.' His voice was bitter but he continued to look warily in the direction of his brother, who had still not spotted them. 'Curtis wouldn't be interested in art if the only other option was a snake pit. For him, art comes on thin paper which can fit into his wallet.'

'That's not entirely fair, Andy,' she said, frowning and snapping her attention back to the man at her side. 'Give him a chance. He's here, isn't he?'

'Yes. So that he can load his gun with more ammunition for another attack on his loser brother.' Underneath the bitterness was a distressing element of pathos, and she noticed that the hand that held his glass was trembling slightly. 'Well, I'm damned if I'll allow him the satisfaction of sneering at me in public.' He swallowed the remainder of his drink. 'I'm off.'

'No, you're not,' she said sharply. 'You're not running away.'

He looked at her hesitantly for a few seconds and then sighed. 'Darling, you *would* remind me of my weaknesses.' She could see him steeling himself for the encounter and loved him for it. She linked her fingers through his and gently squeezed them reassuringly, though, if she were honest, some of that reassurance was for herself as well.

'Well...' He drew in a deep breath. 'Might as well get the ordeal over and done with. Show him the stuff I've done, watch him as he shakes his head sadly at the disappointment I've turned out to be, listen to his lecture on how I'm wasting my talents as a financial consultant for the all important family business and then let him go so he can work on his next attack.'

He raised his arm and waved in the direction of his brother. There was a smile plastered to his face, and Jade obligingly forced one on hers as well. She could feel her heart begin to speed up, and by the time Curtis noticed his brother's frantic waves her nervous system seemed to have joined suit. She licked her lips as he weaved a confident path through the guests, grabbing more than one sidelong glance *en route*. By the time he finally reached them the smile on her face was wearing a bit thin, and the muscles in her jaws were aching.

'What brings you here?' Andy said inanely, and there was a trace of desperation in him as he snatched a couple of glasses of wine from a passing waiter and handed one to Jade. Standing alongside one another, as they were, few would have guessed that they were brothers. This wasn't so much because any actual facial resemblance between them was small but because the personalities reflected on their faces were so completely dissimilar. Both physically handsome, but there was a honed, hard alertness to Curtis which his brother lacked.

'Curiosity,' Curtis said, glancing around him before his eyes resettled onto the two of them. 'Big affair, isn't it? Is that normal for an amateur showing of under-grad work?'

Jade could sense Andy stiffen in response to some hidden meaning behind the remark, but Curtis's voice was supremely polite. She sipped some of the wine in nervous anticipation of where this conversation would end up.

'The college is toying with the idea of introducing art dealers to up-and-coming artists while they're still in the embryonic stage,' Jade contributed hastily. 'They think it serves the dual purpose of getting dealers interested in prospective talent and giving the students a feel of how their work might be viewed once they graduate.'

Curtis inclined his head to one side in an attitude of deep interest, which only served to make her feel more uncomfortable, and drank some of his wine.

'So here's your big chance to become a patron of the arts, big brother, and add another feather to your cap.'

'Or at least familiarise yourself with what we do here,' Jade said, in a fit of excruciating embarrassment at the sarcastic tone in Andy's voice.

'Some of it doesn't look as though it's worth the effort,' Curtis commented, his eyes drifting to the artwork on the walls.

'Broad-minded to the last,' Andy muttered under his breath, his face tightening, and Curtis threw him a cool, shuttered look.

In a minute there'll be an all-out scrap, Jade thought miserably. Right now they were both conducting their conversation in low voices, but Andy had already had a fair amount to drink, and it would take the smallest jibe to provoke him into something far less restrained. He was still insecure about his talents, guilty at the choice he had made even though he could never go back, and, to top it all off, carried a chip on his shoulder about Curtis. It wouldn't take much to ignite the combination, and she had visions of the three of them being chucked out unceremoniously onto the pavement.

'Oh, come on, Andy,' Curtis said with impatience. 'Look at that.' He pointed to the figure of a woman forged out of barbed wire. 'It looks like Aunt Mildred on a bad day.'

Andy, whose shoulders had been hunched in preparation for a fight, relaxed enough to grin reluctantly.

'You mean on a good day, don't you?'

Jade breathed a sigh of relief and finished her glass of wine. Light-headed. Seemed a very good way to be at the moment. She smiled widely at both of them.

'Now that,' Curtis said, moving away slightly and drawing them both with him, 'is quite impressive.' He indicated a small canvas, amidst a collection of similar sizes, which had a deep blue background, splashed with gold at the top and streaked with white at the bottom. The streaks gave it the illusion of movement.

'You like *that*?' Andy gasped. 'I think this calls for another drink.' He signalled to a passing waiter and magnanimously insisted that they all join him. 'Isn't it a bit too *unconventional* for you, big brother?'

Curtis stood in front of the collection and appeared to give the question a great deal of thought. Andy, standing next to him, was frowning, and gulping down his wine with the ferocity of someone intent on slaking a thirst.

'You could be right,' Curtis murmured, straight-faced. 'I know I should stick to rivers and trees...but it's impossible not to admire the way she's slashed her lines across the bottom, as though she's carving the canvas in two, asking us to treat it like separate works. It's very effective.'

'Isn't it?' the man on his left commented. 'Reminiscent, I think, of some paintings from the Modernist movement.'

'Absolutely,' Curtis answered. 'But without the element of self-indulgence.'

The man nodded, and there followed a debate on the relative values of modern art, at the end of which the man strolled off and Curtis looked at them, to see Andy staring at him with open-mouthed surprise.

'Now, that lot over there,' Curtis said, as though the intervening conversation had never occurred, 'is a little too David Hockney for my liking. And where, in all this, are you two?'

Andy, still in gape mode, was too speechless to answer, and Jade nodded to the series of rooms behind him.

Talk about dark horse, she thought. Curtis Greene took the biscuit. No wonder Andy looked as though he had been run over by a steamroller. Not once, since his arrival, had Curtis mentioned even in passing that he took an active interest in art. He had allowed them both to assume that his only interests lay in the world of high finance. She now wondered what else he was keeping up his sleeve. A passion for line dancing? A flair for embroidery? A wife, eight children, two dogs and a goldfish?

'Since I suspect this is the moment you two have been dreading since you were forced to acknowledge me across the room, we might as well amble over and get the ordeal out of the way.'

Andy said something in an unnaturally high-pitched voice and Jade resorted once more to her fund of large, bright smiles.

On the way, he continued to pepper his running conversation with observations on some of the pieces either hanging or standing, and if he noticed that both she and Andy had taken refuge in yet another glass of wine then he gave no indication. It was the only way she found that she could cope with the way the evening was turning out. A week ago she had tossed the invitation at him with no expectation of having it taken up, but, having seen him at the event, she had gritted her teeth, prepared to do battle with her nerves and assumed that there was very little else he could throw at her that he had not thrown at her before. How wrong could she have been?

Still, as he approached Andy's work she felt her stomach clench in anticipation of his dismissal of it. However much bravado Andy displayed when it came to his brother, crushing criticism of what he had done would probably be the most effective way of turning him off art for life.

He moved from canvas to canvas, and in the silence Jade determined to argue the obvious talent in front of them until she turned blue in the face. In fact, she was about to let a bit of the drink do some talking when he turned to them and said simply, 'They're very good.'

'*Good?*' Andy's voice was recriminatory, but his expression told a different story. He was chuffed by his brother's words and was resorting to bluster. '*Good* is very nearly an insult when it comes to evaluating an artist's work. It's almost as bad as describing Mother Teresa as *nice.*'

Curtis looked amused by this. 'I haven't seen any artwork of yours since you were twelve and gave me three of your pictures as a birthday present. I've still got them.'

Which brought a flush of bright red to Andy's cheeks and had him close to choking with embarrassment.

'But you're right,' Curtis went on smoothly. '*Good's* bad. How about thought-provoking? The way you've painted photo-real people in weird settings with abstract backgrounds. Pulls you up short.'

'They're wonderful, aren't they?' Jade said warmly. On the canvas facing her a middle-aged woman, dressed in a fairy's costume, held an iron raised over an ironing board, and behind her birds soared against a translucent blue sky.

'So do I pass the test, big brother?' Andy asked in a hearty voice, with just the smallest shadow of doubt behind it.

'I'll let you know once you've sat the written exam,' Curtis answered drily, and before the conversation could be continued one of the tutors came hurrying up behind him and explained that he had come to drag Andy away.

'Methinks,' Mark Vender said excitedly, 'you have impressed a bigwig with your genius, my lad. How are you enjoying our little parade of talent?' he addressed Curtis, in passing.

'Surpassed expectations,' he said succinctly, and they watched as Andy disappeared through the hall into one of the adjoining side rooms. Jade looked around nervously and wondered how she could manoeuvre an exit. The wine, far too much, had made her feel a little too woolly-headed for her liking. She was getting dangerously close to considering Curtis Greene as *appealing*, which, even in her less than sober frame of mind, was something she knew she should steer well away from.

'And yours?' he asked in a low voice.

'My what?'

'Your work?' he reminded her.

'Oh, please, no,' Jade stammered.

'Why not? I've already seen something of it, or have you forgotten? In my second role as plumber?' He cupped her elbow with his hand and steered her towards the main hall. 'Don't tell me you've suddenly come over all shy about your masterpieces?' he murmured into her ear. She remembered the feel of his mouth on hers and felt a warm flush invade her body.

'Referring to them as *masterpieces* isn't going to have me rushing to show you what I've done,' she responded tartly, before slumping back into dismayed awareness of his hand at her elbow. Out of the corner of her eye she could see various of the students, some of whom she knew, looking at her with interest. No doubt there would be questions as soon as she showed her face in college the following Monday.

Despite the image they liked to create of themselves as free thinkers with a casual, nonchalant attitude to the rest of the human race, people who were above the petty things in life, she knew that they were much the same as everyone else. They loved gossip to a man, and since they had become accustomed to seeing her as the quiet, hardworking one, without much of a wild social life, they would be intrigued at Curtis's presence at her side. What it was like to bathe in the reflected, albeit totally unreal glow of someone else, she thought, smiling weakly at a couple of girls who were on the same course as she was.

'Here we are, then,' she said roughly, standing back just in case he got it into his head to discuss her work with her. 'And please don't say anything,' she ordered, addressing his back and dying to see the expression on his face as he looked at them.

'Not even if it's a compliment?' he asked, back turned away, amusement in his voice.

'I'm no good with compliments.'

'That's not an attractive trait in a woman.' They were still speaking to one another *sotto voce*, and she hoped that no one would amble along too close to realise that. Fortunately the room was clearing. Clumps of people were still standing around, mostly students who were making the most of the last free run of cheap wine, but nearly everyone else was vanishing, probably to get something to eat. Andy was nowhere to be seen, and she decided that that was a good sign. Meant that the bigwig, whoever he might be, was impressed enough to spare more than ten seconds' worth of chat.

'I'm not aiming for attractiveness,' Jade said firmly.

'Course you are; you just don't want to admit it.'

'You never told us that you knew so much about art,' she accused, swerving away from the line of conversation they had been proceeding along.

He had moved closer to the illustrations and was examining them minutely. He couldn't possibly be that interested in them, she thought. He was doing it to get on her nerves.

'Didn't I?'

'No, you didn't. You led us to think that you were a philistine.'

'Correction,' he said, straightening up but not turning to

look at her. 'You arrived at your own conclusions without bothering to find out if you had any evidence to back up your assumptions.'

'A bit like you, then.'

'Touché.' She heard a chuckle in his voice, then he swung round to face her. For a second she had to blink away the illusion that he was even more alarmingly sexy than she recalled from five minutes back. 'So what now?' He looked at her, head tilted, and she stared back at him in bewilderment.

'You like your brother's art. You reassure him that he's done the right thing. You bond with him and then everybody lives happily ever after?'

'Actually, the question was a bit more prosaic than that,' he said wryly. 'I mean, what shall we do now?' He looked at his watch, then back at her. 'I take it Andy's disappeared for the count?'

'Looks that way.' She shifted uncomfortably from foot to foot.

'And my stomach's telling me that it's time to be fed.'

'Then I guess you'd better feed it.'

'I hate eating on my own. I do it when there's no other option, which isn't too often, but really I think that meals for one in restaurants are rather sad affairs. Don't you?'

'I can't say that I've given it much thought,' Jade hedged. She didn't care for the thought of having a meal out with him. Her counsellor had told her that she would need to make the effort, bit by bit, to resume her social life, and she felt that she had come a long way, but dinner with Curtis Greene was going a little too far.

It occurred to her that the only man she had eaten out with for well over two years now was Andy. Ever since Caroline had died, and during that brief but dreadful time when she had nursed her sister, her personal life, she could now see, had been on hold.

She looked at Curtis Greene and wondered what he saw when he looked back at her. He had no idea of the undercurrents flowing through her like toxin. He suspected that there was more to her than met the eye, but suspicions were a long way away from knowledge.

What he would see would be a reasonably attractive fair-haired woman, with enough hang-ups to make her blush whenever he looked at her a bit too hard and enough insecurities to make her hang back at the smallest and most insignificant dinner invitation.

Perhaps he thought that she now considered herself irresistible because he had kissed her. She had *never* overrated her level of attractiveness. Just the opposite. She had unconsciously downplayed it, content to be labelled the brain while Caroline got credit for the looks. She could remember from a very early age all the lavish compliments that had been paid to her sister. Her curly blonde hair had always been gorgeous, her wide blue eyes had always been beautiful, and as she had grown into curvaceous adolescence and her body had taken shape, she had developed a talent for turning heads, the sort of talent that came with a self-confidence that had been lovingly nurtured from childhood.

In the background, Jade had happily hovered, with her straight blonde hair and her brown eyes, veering away from showing off her figure, choosing clothes that camouflaged, and edging away shyly from her sister's gregarious band of friends.

The thought that Curtis Greene, with his supposedly vast experience of the opposite sex, might actually be laughing at her as the plain Jane with an over-sized ego was appalling.

'Are you asking me to have dinner with you?' Jade questioned bluntly. 'Because if you are, then why not? I'm fairly hungry, and anyway, I need something to sop up all the wine I've drunk.'

'Which is the most gracious acceptance of a dinner invitation I've personally heard in a long time.' He grinned at her, and she returned a supercilious little smile.

Adult behaviour was fine, but flirting, she thought, was not on the menu. Not that she felt she had any skills in that particular direction anyway.

'Do you want to find my brother so you can tell him what you're doing?' His eyes were shuttered when he asked this and Jade shook her head.

'If I'm not here when he resurfaces then I expect he'll get the message that I've left.'

'I admire independence in a relationship,' he murmured, moving to guide her towards the exit. 'I've never seen the point of two people who behave as though they were destined to be Siamese twins. Freedom to manoeuvre is very important, wouldn't you agree?'

'No, I don't,' Jade said distractedly, as yet more pairs of curious eyes focused on their journey to the door, 'if what you're suggesting is freedom to sleep with whomever you please whilst involved with someone else.' She succeeded in tugging her hand away on the pretext of brushing her hair out of her face, and, that done, she primly clasped her fingers together around her purse.

'Do I strike you as the sort of man who would do something like that?' he asked, helping her into her coat and watching as she resumed her protective stance.

'I have no idea whether you are or you aren't. I hardly know you at all.'

'Then I assure you that I'm not,' he murmured huskily.

'Now, where would you like to eat? I've lost touch with what's on in London.'

'In which case you're with the wrong person,' Jade said truthfully, stepping out into the freezing night air and gritting her teeth together as the cold seeped through her heavy coat and settled lovingly against her skin. 'I don't do a great deal of eating out, and when I do, it's usually in very cheap places.'

'I thought you said that you had a good job before you chucked it all in?'

'Yes, I did,' Jade answered awkwardly.

In the rush of hailing a taxi, and then deciding where to go, she'd hoped that the issue would be forgotten, but as soon as they were seated in the back of the car he turned to her, leaning his head against the window, and commented neutrally, 'You mean they weren't paying you enough? Was that why you decided to leave and spread your wings doing something completely different?'

'I was being paid very well, as a matter of fact.'

'Then surely you must have wanted to spend your money on good food and clothes and holidays and all the trappings most people work for?'

'No...I...I worked long hours...I was usually too tired at the end of the evening to do anything else but head home, have a shower and slump into bed.' Of all the reasons she could have coughed up for hanging onto her money, she had chosen the most pathetic. Now that she had stuttered out her feeble excuse, she was besieged by thousands of bigger, better and more exciting ones. She risked a glance in his direction, thanking God that the darkness in the taxi prevented him from reading the mortification on her face, and could just about make out his expression of surprise. Or was it pity? Or was it a touch of both?

When he didn't say anything, she could feel herself begin to bristle.

'Go on!' she snapped, folding her arms and glaring at him. 'Why don't you just come right out and say it instead of sitting there…trying not to burst out laughing?'

'Say what?'

'That I'm drab, dreary and hopelessly dull!'

'You're complex, challenging and incredibly sexy.'

Complex? Challenging? Incredibly sexy? Was this his version of sarcasm? It certainly couldn't be the truth because she knew that she was none of those things. She continued to glare witheringly at him while her mind fumbled its way into some kind of order.

'Did you have a nice time at the exhibition?' she asked desperately, and he burst out laughing.

'Very nice, thank you,' he said meekly.

The taxi was pulling up in front of the Italian restaurant which he had recommended, despite the fact that he claimed to have forgotten the London restaurant scene, and almost as soon as it drew to a standstill Jade pulled open the door and more or less tumbled out.

'Here we are. Not the finest, but one of my favourites from way back when. I always make a point of coming here at least once when I get the chance to come to London.' He pulled open the door, stepped aside to allow her to pass, and from under her lashes she quickly scoured his face to see if she could detect any residue of snickering laughter there, but he met her glance with an easy smile and a slight inclination of his head.

'I have an idea to put to you,' he said, as soon as they were seated.

From behind the large, ornate menu, Jade peered at him cautiously.

'And you can stop looking as though any idea I suggest

might involve walking on a bed of nails or jumping through hoops of fire.'

She lowered the menu a few inches and tried to look superior.

'Now that I'm back in London, at least temporarily, and now that I see that Andy isn't about to pack in his art course and return to the bosom of the family company, I think it might be a good idea if we do something...along family lines.' He appeared to find this description lacking, because he frowned, and then continued, taking his time, 'It was something of a tradition, on New Year's Eve, for our parents to throw a huge party at their house in Scotland for all their friends. Admittedly I've lost touch with some of them, and true New Year's Eve has come and gone, but it occurred to me while we were walking around the exhibition that something lavish might be nice. I've been away for a long time. Andy barely knows the Scotland house...what better?'

'Why are you asking for my opinion?'

'Because,' he explained with exaggerated patience, 'you're going to be the one to convince Andy that it's a good idea. It's time we healed rifts, and a party of old friends and new might be amusing, to say the least. I can get the housekeeper there to sort the place out, get bedrooms ready, and we can fix it for two weeks' time.'

'What happens at these parties?' Jade asked faintly, putting down the menu.

'A long weekend of good food, good wine, some fishing if the weather permits.'

'It's winter!'

'Best time to be in Scotland,' he said, amused at her look of horror. 'Bracing. Toughens you up.'

'Well, yes, all right, I'll suggest it to Andy...' It *was* a good idea. Getting to know one another would be easier, she supposed, in the company of other people. Less opportunity to lock horns.

'And naturally I expect you to be there,' he added casually, signalling for a waiter to come and take their order.

'Me? Why? I'm not part of your family.'

'Tut, tut, tut. Now don't downplay the role you occupy in my brother's life. Andy can invite some of his other friends; you won't be walking around in a daze of unfamiliarity. Besides...' he shot her a winning smile '...you'll be playing hostess.'

CHAPTER FIVE

JADE looked at Andy and then groaned aloud.

Thinking about it, there had been several pointers that Curtis's little scheme was not going to go smoothly, and this was now the icing on the cake.

To begin with the idea had been greeted with lukewarm scepticism by Andy, who had announced that he barely knew any of the names of the old family friends who'd used to frequent their parents' parties.

'You seem to forget, big brother,' he'd said with unfailing tactlessness, 'that by the time Sarah and I arrived on the scene their interest in us was strictly on the nominal side. I remember my teachers at boarding school a damn sight better than I remember any of their Scottish fellow trend-setters. Anyway, they're probably all dead, or else old and decrepit.'

Which had opened up yet another simmering family argument, culminating in an enraged Curtis bellowing that it was time his brother grew up and Andy storming out of the room.

Jade, who now no longer seemed to have the time to dwell on her own problems, had taken on the role of inveterate peacemaker, tossed as she was in the middle of these hostilities, and it had taken the cunning of a fox to bring them both back down to earth. At one point she was reduced to yelling, *'Shut up!'* at the top of her lungs, simply to quell the never-ending string of accusations and counter-accusations.

'You,' she had said, standing at the dinner table with her

finger pointed at Curtis, who had glowered but remained silent, 'can hardly accuse your brother of acting like a child when you're barely doing any better yourself!

'And you,' she had continued, before he could find the power of speech, pointing at Andy, 'will have to come to terms with the fact that you can't go through life without compromise.'

That said, she had sat back down, serenely finished her cup of coffee, and watched with a feeling of satisfaction as they'd groped their way through their bull-headedness towards a solution. Old family friends, most of whom would, Curtis had agreed with a wry grin, collapse with surprise should they receive an invitation from him after so many years, would not be invited. He wouldn't, on reflection, he'd said piously, be responsible for endangering anyone's health.

Instead, Andy would ask ten of his closest friends and Curtis would ask five friends and five of the company directors, who would greatly appreciate the gesture. They had both then looked at her and suggested that, since fair was fair, she should ask ten of hers, to which she had politely declined. Did she have ten? They seemed to have dwindled away over the weeks and months and years.

That hurdle successfully jumped, and with all the invitations accepted, they had then discovered that Jesse, the housekeeper, was having her daughter up from Devon over that weekend and so wouldn't be able to sleep over. Whereupon Curtis's powers of persuasion had come into play, so that they had finally agreed that not only would Jesse sleep in, but also her daughter and her two youngest sons, who couldn't possibly remain on their own for the duration of the four days.

'Will there be enough room in the house for all these people?' she had asked Curtis dubiously, envisaging a moderately large place bursting at the seams with a collection of people who would probably be at each other's throats after day one.

'Jesse will open up one of the wings.'

'Ah,' Jade had said, nodding with a dry expression. 'Naturally. God, those extra wings are useful when it comes to house parties, aren't they?'

Ever since the exhibition, and Curtis's acceptance of his brother's lifestyle, or at least his visible acceptance of it, he had been keeping his tendency for razor-sharp sarcasm under control. They were now actually managing to have dinners when the conversation trundled along in a fairly amicable way, even though Jade still kept as low a profile as she could.

She told herself that that was simply because she wanted to give the brothers all the space they needed to get to know one another, without intrusion from a third party. But she was uneasily aware that the truth was far more complex than that. She wanted to keep her distance from Curtis for her own sake. Now that he was no longer on the attack, that charm which she had glimpsed occasionally was dangerously apparent, and it lay not in any deliberate attempt to flirt with her but in his personality. He charmed men and women alike. He had the sort of sharp, incisive wit that could force a grin out of a confirmed battleaxe and a talent for persuasiveness that she had never encountered before. Little by little, he was drawing his brother out of himself, easing the chip away from his shoulder, and when Andy's inclination to be defensive rose to the surface, she could almost see Curtis speculating on the best possible way of dealing with it.

Holding on to her common sense and ingrained need for self-protection were the two pieces in her armoury which she pulled out of the cupboard whenever his eyes turned to her and his charm began worming its way into her secrets.

Now, she looked at Andy over her cup of tea in the college cafeteria with dismay.

'You can't do this to me!' She dropped her head into the palm of her hand and gave another groan of despair.

'Why,' he asked, reasonably enough, 'are you getting so worked up over it? It's not as though I won't be coming. I just won't be travelling with you two a day ahead of schedule as we'd arranged. So where's the problem? You have to admit that I've been an angel over the whole thing, agreeing to go along with it even at the expense of my poor friends, who are going to be bored to tears having to socialise with a bunch of stuffy businessmen.' He crammed some more jam doughnut into his mouth and then looked a little startled when the jam oozed down his fingers.

'Well, I don't see why *I* should travel up to Scotland alone with your brother. I'm not *part* of the family...'

'Ah, but you're going to be playing the little hostess. You have to be on hand from day one to do all those little hostessy things that big brother will expect. Check all the rooms. Do interesting things with vases and bunches of flowers.' He finished the remainder of the doughnut in one mouthful and then used four napkins to wipe his mouth. 'Make sure you pack hostessy clothes as well. Jeans are going to be right out of the question.'

Jade hadn't given the wardrobe side of things much thought, but now she frowned and looked worried. She didn't know what clothes she was going to take for this affair. Andy's friends would all wear their usual garb of denim and black, and the stuffy businessmen and their wives would probably wear blazers and ties and starched daffodil-yellow knee-length skirts with matching jackets and pearls. Whichever camp she chose to go into, she would be left looking either too informal or else ridiculously overdressed and stuffy.

Too late now to bemoan the role she had found herself in. Curtis had manoeuvred the situation very cleverly. When he had announced to her that she would be playing hostess he had obviously expected her shriek of horror and flat-out refusal to do any such thing, because instead of being taken aback he had simply swerved course and attacked her from another angle.

He was surprised, he had said, and a little disappointed that she refused to help out in a situation like this, when he was trying to build bridges. It wasn't as though she had no experience of doing that kind of thing. She had surely been present at the odd client function in her career as 'Very Important Personal Assistant' at her last job, hadn't she? Had probably seen some things through from start to finish? Wasn't he correct? He'd claimed not to know how things were handled over here in London, but he had succeeded in forcing her either to confess to having worked in a tin pot company and lying about her status there or else to admit that, yes, she *had* helped her boss in hosting various company parties.

He had shrugged negligently, as though bemused by her refusal, and had then proceeded to point out how crucial it would be having someone to oversee events tactfully—after all, businessmen and artists were a potentially combustible union. But naturally, despite the fact that she was living in his house rent-free, she was perfectly at liberty not to help out on the one occasion he requested. After all, she could do as she pleased. No one was going to hold a gun to her head.

In the end, she had found herself agreeing.

'You'll have to wear your power suits by day and demure little numbers by night,' Andy continued. 'Nothing too startling. You don't want to have the businessmen leering at you while their wives hover resentfully in the background. You'll have to be on best behaviour, lots of smiles and jollying everyone along when things look as though they're getting awkward. You'll love it!'

'It's going to be a nightmare.'

'But for such a good cause! Two brothers uniting!'

'Don't be so cynical, Andy. You *know* you're secretly pleased that Curtis has accepted your decision without too much blood being spilled.'

'There's still a lot he doesn't know about me, Jade.'

'Yes, well, give it time,' she said hastily. 'And stop distracting me from feeling furious with you for *backing out* and leaving me to go up *alone* with your brother!'

'Just giving you two the chance to get to know one another. Don't think I haven't seen the way he looks at you.' When she gave him a thunderous glare, he continued quickly, 'Anyway, I can't help it if Bigwig Lucas has set up an appointment to view some of my work when I'm supposed to be taking a plane to Scotland. I can hardly tell him to rearrange his schedule to suit me.' He pressed one finger to the plate, so that some of the sugar from the doughnut adhered to his skin, and he sucked it off, repeating the exercise until the plate looked as though it had been put through the dishwasher.

The prospect of time alone with Curtis Greene loomed before her eyes like the vision of a volcano, teetering on the brink of possible eruption.

The airport, alone. The plane trip, alone. Then the rambling mansion, big enough for the housekeeper and her entourage to conveniently get lost in while they ate, alone. Lots of alones to fill, she thought despondently, wondering, as the day progressed, how much small talk she was capable of raking up for the occasion.

She felt sick at the thought of what a handful of hours might hold in store for her. There was always the chance that he would revert to his Spanish Inquisition routine about her motives. Although to be fair he seemed to have dropped that particular angle, since it was glaringly obvious that, however close she and Andy were, they were not lovers. More worryingly, he might find isolation the perfect time to start needling her about her private life, something which continued to interest him, judging from his knack of firing personal questions at her under the ludicrous guise of absent-minded curiosity. As though she had been born yesterday and couldn't see through his ploy. He still wanted to get to the bottom of her, and in the presence of his brother there was a limit to how much he could reasonably ask without appearing boorishly inquisitive. The scenario presenting itself contained no convenient chaperones to ward off his questions.

Her only hope, she thought, was if Curtis came to the conclusion that it made sense for them all to delay their plans for one day and then travel together as previously arranged.

It was a hope destined to be shot down in flames before it even had time to take root.

'Too bad,' he greeted Andy's explanation. 'Might work out for the best, though. Jade and I go on ahead, leaving you to sort out the lot down here, get them to the house in one piece. I take it,' he said silkily, turning to her, 'that you're not bothered by my brother's defection?'

Later, after Andy had left the room, Jade stayed behind, a first, and hesitantly watched Curtis as he sipped from his coffee and watched her back, in no hurry to rescue her by initiating any conversation. Eventually, she said, 'About this weekend...'

He continued to look at her across the dining table with lazy interest, allowing the silence to engulf them. Like most people who are accustomed to running the show and are highly self-confident, he was not in the least fazed by silence. He never filled pauses with inanities simply for the sake of talking.

'What role am I supposed to have? I mean…what sort of clothes should I be bringing with me? It's just that I gave away most of my work clothes to charity when I gave up my job…' It had been a gesture of freedom, and she had thoroughly enjoyed chucking the lot into a black bin bag and taking it to the nearest charity shop. Little could she have foreseen that she might need some of them sooner than she'd thought.

'No need for suits,' he said, amused. 'You won't be *working*, just helping me out. Wear what you would normally wear for smartish occasions.' He frowned. 'You don't have to impress anyone, you know.'

'No, I realise that…'

'You're not *nervous*, are you?'

His question caught her on the hop, and she didn't have time to think of a suitably dismissive denial. Instead, she paused for a few seconds with her lips parted, giving him ample time to nudge his way in with a few speculations of his own.

'You *are* nervous. Why?'

'B-Because…' she stammered, furious at being pinned to the wall, but realising that her hesitation after his question had been long enough to give the lie to any denials she might now come up with. 'The only real socialising I've done over the past couple of years has been to do with work. I…I've been so busy and…I'm not sure if I'll be any good at…' Her voice was practically inaudible now, and finally petered out altogether.

Having burrowed this deep, she expected him to plunge right in and carry on digging, but instead he looked at her for a few brief seconds, then said kindly, 'Sarah used the house quite a bit before she went to Australia. It's more than likely that she left some clothes in the room she used to sleep in. Knowing my sister, probably more than just a few,' he amended wryly, 'and she's more or less your size. I'm sure she wouldn't mind if you borrowed what you wanted.'

'Good!' She sprang out of the chair, anxious now to be out of the room.

She was pulling open the door to leave when he said softly, from behind her, 'There's really no need to be nervous. You presumably know all of the people Andy's invited, and my lot may not wear odd clothes and live out of knapsacks, but they're really quite a relaxed bunch. No one's going to be looking to pick holes, and if anyone asks too many questions…well…' he gave her a slow, heat-inducing smile '…you can always dodge them. You're good at that.'

His reassurances should have put some of her nerves to rest, but whichever set of nerves that was, another larger set had been resolutely activated by that smile of his. However much she told herself that he had not singled her out for any special blast of Curtis Greene charm, there had been occasions when the air between them throbbed with electricity. She didn't know if it stemmed from his curiosity, his desire to goad her into a response, or if it was simply a game he unconsciously played whenever he was in the presence of a reasonably attractive member of the opposite sex, but his languid, ambiguous teasing left her floundering.

She could deal with his bare-face arrogance, and even the outlandish accusations he had hurled at her when he had first revealed his identity, but she was vulnerable when it came to anything else. She wouldn't have been in the least bit surprised if he suspected as much and had decided to deliberately pull her secrets out of her stealthily, but that didn't matter. What mattered was that she felt as though she didn't dare drop her guard, not for a minute, when she was with him.

She awoke at six o'clock on the morning of their flight, and was so wrapped up in last-minute packing and an anxious examination of the things she had stuffed into the suitcase that she didn't notice the weather until she pulled back the curtains one hour later.

The sky was the colour of lead. Through the window, she could feel the intense cold struggling to push into the room, where it would make short work of the central heating. If it was like this in London, how much colder would it be in Scotland? She had never been nearly as far north as that, and she naively suspected that even when the rest of the country basked in summer sunshine Scotland steadfastly refused to bend to peer pressure and simply remained freezing cold, whatever the season.

'Have you seen the sky?' was her opening question, when she lugged her case downstairs to find Curtis waiting for her in the hall.

'Are you sure you've packed enough?' He eyed her small case dubiously.

'We're going for four days,' Jade said, distracted, 'not two weeks.' His case, alarmingly, was twice the size of hers. 'How much stuff *are* you taking?' she asked, circling the Louis Vuitton case on the ground as though it was some foreign and slightly bewildering species of animal.

'Enough to get by.'

'You mean with a change of outfit every twenty minutes?'

'I mean,' he said patiently, 'with several jumpers for those healthy outdoor pursuits, such as walking and exploring the isolated countryside.'

Which neatly brought her back to her original subject.

'It looks as if it's going to snow, and if it snows here, God knows what the state of Scotland will be.'

'No snow predicted on the weather reports,' he told her cheerfully, taking both cases and allowing her to open the front door for him. 'And even if it snowed twelve inches here, there's no guarantee that it'll be worse up north. Weather fronts are a bit more unpredictable than that.'

For all the world as if he knew the first thing about them. He was a businessman, unless he had been keeping a useful degree in meteorology up his sleeve. However, since she wouldn't have put it past him to produce a diploma in weather forecasting, she refrained from continuing the subject, only noting to herself that the ominous sky was yet another sign that this trip had been a bad idea from the word go.

The traffic was sluggish. Curtis had arranged for his driver to collect them, and Jade sat in the back seat, gloomily staring out of the window and internally taking bets that the first flake of snow would hit the ground before they even made it to the airport. Next to her, Curtis lounged with his hands behind his head, perfectly relaxed and apparently dozing.

'Anyway,' he said out of the blue, making her jump because she had thought him safely asleep, 'why are you so afraid of a little snow? *Everyone* likes snow. Little children build snowmen and adults turn back into little children and build snowmen. It's a well-documented phenomenon.' He grinned, and half closed his eyes again.

'I can't imagine *you* as a little child,' Jade muttered under her breath.

'And I thought women always saw the boy behind the man. Now I'm disillusioned.' He opened one eye, then shut it back when satisfied that he had engendered the desired response of blushing discomfort in her.

She was fast accepting that being stuck with him overnight in some rambling mansion in the wilds of Scotland was going to be even worse than she had originally imagined, especially if he intended to do away with polite formality and spend the entire time in banter mode.

'That's probably because most men refuse to grow up.'

'Oh, I don't know about that. You treat Andy like a little boy, yet you have to admit he was grown up enough to make some pretty big decisions about his life.'

'Andy's vulnerable...' she found herself saying, and, as expected, he was quick to jump in.

'And I'm not?' Both blue eyes were now wide open, and inspecting her face with devilish amusement. 'If you care to look, I happen to be a very vulnerable human being, Jade.'

'Well, I *don't* care to look,' she answered with haughty indifference.

'Oh, yes, you do. You're bursting with curiosity, just like I am about you. Why don't you admit it? Human beings are far more similar in nature than we like to admit. We're all prone to exactly the same emotions. They merely differ in proportion from one person to another. I mean,' he said lazily, 'let's just say that, speaking purely hypothetically, *you* would dearly love to get to know me better...'

She gave a snort at that.

'...you'd go out of your way to pretend that the feeling didn't exist. Whereas another woman might pursue her interest a lot more openly... Right into the bed, in fact.'

If he hadn't added that little postscript, she might have thought that he was being serious. The minute he brought the mention of bed into his little soliloquy, she knew that he was playing with her. He wanted to see what kind of reaction he would provoke, and the more she reacted with embarrassed horror at his forthrightness, the more tempted he would be to play his games.

'Thank you for sharing that with me,' she told him, hoping he would notice that she wasn't even bothering to favour him with a look. 'Also for informing me that I'm secretly dying to get to know you. Because until you said it, I had no idea that I was.'

He laughed, and was still laughing to himself when the driver pulled up at one of the entrances to the airport, inclining his body to listen to the list of instructions that Curtis was rattling off to him. As was often the case in London, the sky, which had gleefully threatened snow, had failed to deliver, although it was still freezing cold, and she wrapped her coat tightly around her, pulling the collar up against the sides of her face and hurrying behind Curtis. It was even chilly inside the airport, chilly enough for her to keep her coat on, although once he had checked in he removed his black trench coat and slung it over one arm.

'We don't have long to board,' he informed her. 'Anything you want to get before we fly? Perfume? Chocolates? Barbour to protect you from the biting cold when we go on our long nature rambles?'

'Magazines.'

'Why?' He stopped walking and frowned, perplexed. 'You won't have any time to read them. Between the cross-country hikes, the trips to the kitchen overseeing the food and the nerve-racking mingling to make sure that everyone has a good time you won't have a minute to yourself, never mind relaxing with a stack of magazines.'

'Very funny.' She ignored his remarks, browsed for a few minutes by the magazine racks, very much aware of him hovering behind her, and resisted the temptation to whack him across the ear with the copy of *Cosmopolitan* in her hand when he began making ridiculous remarks about some of the articles on the front covers.

'What's a G-spot?' he asked her innocently, which attracted a few amused titters from the two teenage girls behind them in the queue.

'Groin,' Jade hissed back. 'It's the famous *Groin Spot*, and you'd better cover yours before it comes into contact with my knee!'

Her feathers firmly ruffled, he subsided into docility, and allowed her to read her magazine in peace as they settled into their seats on the plane. He reached inside his bag, which was big but had fortunately escaped qualifying for the hold, and pulled out a book. After a few sidelong glances, she finally rested her magazine face-down on her lap and said, 'You're reading.'

'Oh, yes, so I am,' he told her in a surprised voice, turning the book round in his big hands as though noticing it for the first time.

'A novel.'

'I know,' he apologised. 'I do sometimes take a break from reading work documents. It's out of character for a top businessman, but there you have it. Once in a while, I read books.'

'It's a *feminist* novel,' Jade accused. 'I've read most of hers.'

'So you read too? We have something in common. Isn't that a reassuring thought?' He leaned back and closed his eyes, a smile tugging the corners of his mouth. 'It's a bit tamer than your magazine, though,' he murmured. 'Not a single mention of any G-spots. I might just have to borrow that magazine from you when we get to Scotland.'

'Why?' Jade asked tartly. 'You won't have time to read

it. You'll be too busy taking long, bracing walks and mingling with all your guests.' The smile grew broader and she
took refuge behind the magazine, glancing up only to order
a drink, then remembering, when she looked back down at
what she was reading, that she hadn't read a word for the
past ten minutes. She hastily turned a few pages, but her
mind was whizzing around in frantic circles.

Six months ago, if someone had told her that she would
be sitting on a plane, on a flight to Glasgow, next to a man
who could make her hackles rise and have her heart leap-
frogging all in the space of one minute, she would have
shaken her head in disbelief. Whether she cared to admit it
or not, it was becoming clear that her trance-like preoccu-
pation with herself was splintering into more and more
pieces with every passing day. She still thought of her sister, but the thoughts were now more focused on the glorious
things they had done together before she had become ill,
and less on the black times when her diagnosis had left
them both facing the certainty of her premature death.

Was this what her counsellor had referred to as *picking
up the pieces of her life*? If it was, then she was torn between resenting the feeling and thriving on it, like someone
relearning the painful process of walking after a terrible car
accident. Each step hurt, but as she sat there, not reading
the article on *Men After Divorce*, she realised, with surprise,
that the steps were getting less and less painful with every
passing day. She folded shut the magazine with trembling
hands and turned her head away from Curtis. She half expected him to interrupt the silence, but when she sneaked
a glance at him it was to find him reading, his brow creased
in thoughtful concentration.

She resumed her mental pacing, but she knew that her
thoughts were going nowhere. Every time she tried to grasp
one long enough to analyse it, it skittered away out of reach

and she was left holding thin air. In the end she closed her eyes and thought about her art. She hadn't had as much success as Andy, but she knew that he needed it far more than she did. The success of an artist was an intangible mixture of talent and luck. As an illustrative artist, she would be far more commercially secure when her course was completed. Her tutor had said as much. It was just as well, because she, unlike Andy, had no cushion of family wealth to fall back on. Taking time out was going to be an expensive enough venture as it was, without having to tackle the prospect of unemployment when she emerged, qualified.

She was beginning to doze off on her thoughts when she felt the plane begin to dip and the announcement came on that seat belts were to be fastened.

Then another announcement.

It was snowing.

'I knew it,' Jade said, peering around Curtis's bulk to stare out of the window—a pointless exercise since all she could make out was the dense grey of the clouds. They were still too high up for her to see what the weather on the ground was like, but a mental calculation of what she had packed was enough to convince her that her jumper quotient was not up to any severe weather conditions.

It now occurred to her that perhaps the house wasn't centrally heated. Lots of roaring open fires, but no central heating. Old houses, especially ones with wings, were notoriously lacking in the essential comforts. Hadn't she read that somewhere? Twenty Londoners, politely trying to play down the chattering of their teeth, with only the odd log fire and glasses of brandy to keep them warm. Not only would they not get along, they would also spend the entire four days in a state of semi-permanent inebriation from drinking too much brandy.

The plane began to descend, and it was only when they were safely on the ground that Curtis turned to her and said, with a Gallic shrug of his massive shoulders. ''You got your snow, it seems!'

'It's...it's a blizzard!' Jade squeaked, when they were outside the airport.

'It's not a *blizzard*,' he said, glancing around him. 'I arranged with Jack to leave the Land Rover at a very good hotel in the city centre...' The snow was collecting on his coat, fine, white and persistent, and he carelessly brushed some of it off. 'I thought we might have a bite to eat before we begin the drive to the house. We need a taxi.'

We need snow suits, Jade thought, looking at the pelting snow worriedly. Within a few minutes they got their taxi, which was blessedly warm, and Curtis relaxed with a deep sigh.

'It's a beautiful city. Did you know that it was voted the City of Culture in 1990? It's had its bad times, of course, but it's pulled through remarkably well. I've always tried to make it up here when I've been in London. Occasionally, when I've needed a rest, I've bypassed London completely and just headed up here to crash out. This is reputedly the finest Victorian city in Britain. Course, I'm biased. Most of my formative years were spent in Scotland. I know the area we'll be going to like the back of my hand, and, believe it or not, I've kept in touch with quite a few of the locals. Always make sure that I visit them when I'm over.'

He sighed with contentment, and Jade tried very hard not to notice that the snow seemed to be getting heavier. The beautiful Victorian architecture was laced with white, and progress in the taxi was painfully slow.

When they finally reached their temporary destination, the first thing Curtis did was ensure that the Land Rover was parked in the hotel car park.

'How far do we have to drive?' Jade asked, hurrying behind him into the hotel.

'Not too far. An hour or so.'

'An hour! *An hour!*'

'No need for alarm. The car and I are quite used to these rugged conditions. That's the problem with you Londoners. You're just too soft.' He began walking towards the foyer, and she tugged his sleeve urgently.

'I think we should get going,' she said firmly. 'Look at the weather!' He duly looked out of the revolving doors. '*You* might be used to these so-called "rugged conditions", but *I'm* not, and I don't fancy a drive out of the city centre in it.'

He sighed and shook his head. 'Well, if it would make you happier...'

'I would be as chipper as a cricket.'

'...although Land Rovers *can* tackle most weather conditions. They're designed for hard driving.'

'I don't care if they're designed to cope with avalanches. I'd just feel better if we got there in one piece.'

He gave her an amused smile, but she was relieved when he nodded his head.

After one and a half hours, during which they had left the bustle of city life long behind and were now travelling at a snail-like pace through a landscape of white, with the snow getting heavier by the second, he said, under his breath, 'Not too far now.'

'How far?'

They could be anywhere, she thought. The moon. The snow made nonsense of landmarks, but for some reason she trusted him utterly not to get lost.

Another hour later they finally drove into a village, and he said, with relief, 'Almost there now. This is the local village. The house is just fifteen minutes along. I'll just pull into old Tom's guest house and catch my breath for half an hour. My eyes feel as though I've been up for ten hours after a hard night, and we can grab something to eat.'

At least they only had a few more minutes of this snow, because Jade, personally, didn't think they could go much further. At times the snow had impacted so thickly onto the windscreen that he had been obliged to get out of the car and manually clear it away before continuing.

He gingerly parked the car outside the guest house, which was a Victorian detached house, noticeable as a guest house only because of the sign outside.

'Tom and I go back a long way,' Curtis said, as they made their slow way up the path. 'He used to do odd jobs around the house when business was a bit low and his wife could keep the place going without him. Old Tom and I have spent many an illuminating hour talking about life.' There was a smile in his voice that made her smile as well.

'Dare I ask what the subject of these illuminating conversations was?'

'Sex,' Curtis murmured gravely. 'A very important topic to a teenage boy.'

She felt a tingle at the single word, which could generate so many split-second erotic images when Curtis said it.

'He'll be pleased to see us.'

'Curtis Greene! Ye old rogue!' An old man with grey hair and the dapper appearance of someone who still enjoyed shopping for clothes emerged from behind the reception counter. His eyes had lit up into two bright slits of friendly welcome. 'The good lady and I thought that you might stop here, and thank the heavens you did, laddie!'

'Don't tell me you got Rose to cook my special steak and kidney pie, Tom!'

'And a bit more!'

'A bit more?' Jade, who had sidled into the background

during this hearty interchange, now scuttled out a little, smiling as introductions were made.

'Aye, wee lass.' He nodded. 'You'll be sampling some fine Scottish fare here for the next few days.' He cackled and shook with laughter. 'Road to the house is completely blocked! So you and your bonny lassie will have to make do with the room here tonight, and I shouldn't get too excited about leaving in a hurry! More snow on the way!' He beamed as though he had just imparted the good news that they had won the Lottery. 'You have to admit, son, that this Scotland of ours never changes!'

CHAPTER SIX

'THIS is ridiculous!'

Jade stood with her back to the closed bedroom door and her hands on her hips.

'I wouldn't say that...' Curtis looked around the bedroom slowly, then tested the bed with his hand. 'I agree it's not very big, but I think it's quite tastefully furnished, and there *is* an *en suite* bathroom. The mattress feels all right as well.'

'You know what I mean!' she burst out, absolutely refusing to see anything funny about the situation.

His response to that was to flop onto the bed, kick off his shoes and lie back with his hands behind his head. With his eyes closed, he looked the picture of sleeping innocence. Anyone would think that the man hadn't a care in the world.

'And you can stop looking so...so *relaxed*!' she spluttered furiously.

He opened one eye to look at her. 'Well, there's not much we can do about the situation, is there? So what's the point getting worked up about it?'

'You *could* have made more of an effort *not* to land us in this situation, then we wouldn't be here now, getting worked up about it!'

'*You're* the only one who seems worked up.' He rolled to his side to look at her, propping himself up by his elbow.

'Can you blame me?' She took a couple of steps into the room to glare down at him. '*This* is hardly what I expected!' On the sofa by the bay window their luggage stared back at her, an insolent reminder of what lay ahead unless she did something to change the situation.

It had been bad enough to discover that there was no way forward to the house, and that with weather reports promising more snow the party would have to be cancelled, but from that point things had rapidly gone downhill.

With a great deal of suggestive remarks, Tom had revealed that he could put them up in *a* room, but there was no chance of separate rooms because the remaining four were taken. More unfortunate travellers who had ventured this far but could go no further. Jade's expression of speechless horror had been lost on him, not least because he had blithely assumed that she and Curtis were together, in every sense of the word, an impression which Curtis had not hastened to dispel.

'It's no good you lying there. You're going to have to go and sort something out, because I'm not sharing this room with you. And this is all your fault. We should have stayed put in the city, checked into some rooms at the hotel, but, oh, no, you and that Land Rover could tackle any amount of snow, couldn't you? Arctic conditions? No problem! Just an everyday affair for a big, sturdy, four-wheel drive car at the hands of a macho hulk! And it's not funny!' she yelled, when she saw that his shoulders were shaking with mirth.

'I got you here, didn't I?' he sobered up enough to point out. 'Many more wimpish men than myself would have shrivelled up under the challenge, but you have to admit that, macho hulk that I am, I did barge my way through blizzards to make it here safely and in one piece.'

'Well, you can barge your way downstairs and sort some alternative sleeping arrangements out!'

'You can hardly expect Tom to chuck someone out to fit in with what *you* want,' he said with implacable calm.

'Besides, he would find it very odd that you want to sleep in a different room. He might jump to the conclusion that we'd had a lovers' tiff, and then you'd have to fabricate something to keep the lie going and it would all get very tedious and complicated.'

'You should have told him from the start that we weren't…weren't… When I tried to explain, you could have backed me up instead of talking over me!'

'I could have…but Tom mentioned that he had already turned away two couples, directed them to the local rectory to see whether the vicar could put them up some-how…which means that he held this room for us as soon as he realised that we might need it. If I'd told him that we needed two separate rooms, it would have thrown him into a tizzy.

'He's a good man, good enough to do something stupid like bring their teenage son into their room with them to oblige me, and I wasn't having anything of the sort.' His face was hard. 'And I'd better make it clear to you that you keep your prim scruples to yourself. As far as Tom and Rose are concerned, you and I are lovers, and they've done us the most enormous favour by saving this room for us. Which, incidentally, they have.'

'Maybe we could try and make it to the house,' she suggested, clutching at one final straw, and he gave a bark of laughter as though she had suddenly and mysteriously taken leave of her senses.

'*Make it to the house?* Are you completely mad?'

'Well, if it's only a few minutes' drive away…!' Jade retorted heatedly, feeling a fool for having suggested it in the first place.

'At least fifteen minutes, and, rugged though the Land Rover may be, it would need wings to get it over the snow-drifts! Of course, if you're *that* hell-bent on not sharing this room, you could always try and leg it to the house. If you give me a piece of paper, I could draw you a little map. Oh, no, why bother with a map? You wouldn't be able to see the road anyway, with this snow. It's just a straight line to the house, before the left-hand turn and the steep hill.'

Which left very little to say.

He stretched out his hand, still lying down, which forced her to take up residence on the sofa by the bay window, from which she gloomily stared outside at the relentless fall of snow, and pulled the telephone onto his broad chest.

She listened as he called his brother, then the various directors and friends, leaving messages in some instances, informing them that the weather had sabotaged the party.

'It's snowing in London,' he announced, turning to look at her. 'Pretty heavily. As it turns out, they would have probably had problems getting here.'

Jade didn't say anything. She desperately wanted a bath, but the thought of being naked only feet away from him, albeit behind a firmly locked door, made her feel a little ill. Nor did she want to unpack her few belongings while he lay there on the bed in that Lord of the Manor pose, surveying her. Why didn't he do the sociable thing and go downstairs and chat to his mentor, Tom? They hadn't seen each other in a few months. Surely they must have *something* to catch up on! If conversation dried up, she thought viciously, he could always launch into some rhetoric on his sexual exploits as a way of saying a big thank you to Tom for his illuminating chats on the facts of life twenty years previously.

'Why don't you go and have a bath?' he said, either reading her mind or else deciding to plunge into the growing silence and coincidentally hitting on what she had been thinking herself. 'You look fairly bedraggled.'

'You don't exactly look like something off the cover of

Vogue yourself,' Jade told him acidly. Right now, she blamed him for everything. The weather, the fact that the road to the house was closed, the fact that Tom only had one vacant room. How could he be so cool and collected while she sat here with a churning stomach and thoughts about that one bed which she couldn't even bring herself to formulate?

She turned her back to him, shielding his eyes from what she was doing, and busily rummaged through her case, extracting a pair of knickers, some black trousers and a grey and black ribbed jumper which had been destined to be one of her casual-yet-not-as-casual-as-jeans outfits.

'I'm going to do just that,' she said loudly. Maybe he was so exhausted after his driving that he would do her the favour of falling asleep. Maybe for several days, or however long it took for the snow to clear. Never mind that he seemed depressingly bright-eyed and bushy-tailed at the moment.

She edged around the bed, which seemed to take up an inordinate amount of space in the bedroom, averting her eyes from the blatantly erotic image presented by a spread-eagled Curtis, and once in the bathroom noisily locked the door behind her.

She would take a very long time having a bath. She needed to think.

They couldn't possibly share that bed. It was out of the question. Nor, she reluctantly admitted to herself, could either of them approach Tom to find out whether he could accommodate one of them somewhere else. He was a kind, thoughtful man who clearly had a great deal of affection of Curtis, for reasons which were frankly beyond her comprehension, and she had a gut feeling that Curtis had not been lying when he'd said that Tom would inconvenience himself rather than cause either of them embarrassment or distress. The thought of Curtis Greene being distressed over anything made her snort sourly, but she didn't want to cause trouble to someone whom she had instinctively liked and who had kindly kept the room free for them both.

She ran a deep bath, stripped off, and then subsided into the foamy water, where she intended to remain for as long as possible. Through the narrow window opposite she could see the snow swirling down from the heavens. There was something dreamy about that, and under different circumstances, with a different man, someone with whom she *was* involved, she imagined that the scenario would have been a deliciously romantic one. Marooned in a charming guest house, with the snow pelting down outside, lots of hearty winter food and then the toasty cosiness of the king-size bed with its feather mattress and fluffy duvet.

She gave a soft moan of pleasure at the thought of it, remembered the identity of her uninvited companion and immediately began soaping herself vigorously.

When she emerged forty minutes later, fully dressed, it was to find the bedroom empty. The bed still showed the indentation of his long body, something which she immediately rectified by pulling straight the duvet and plumping up the pillows. It crossed her mind that she could arrange a makeshift bed for him on the ground, somewhere preferably out of her line of vision, but just in case he returned she decided to put his unexpected absence to greater use.

She quickly unpacked her case, hanging up the three dresses she had brought with her, though why she was bothering she had no idea. This was not the sort of place that required little black cocktail numbers for dinner. Her nightie, which was really an oversized tee shirt, she placed on top of the pillows, bang in the middle of them, staking her territory while she had the chance. Her make-up she arranged on the bathroom shelf.

Then she made her way downstairs.

The informal bar area was fairly full with other guests, immediately identifiable by their conspicuous lack of appropriate clothing, and what could only be regulars. The roads were thickly covered with snow, but not so thick that a brief walk outside wasn't possible, and the guest house, situated as it was in the middle of the village, was in a prime location for locals whose thirst for beer had not been dampened by the weather.

In the corner she saw Curtis, standing by the bar with a pint glass in his hand, chatting to Tom over the counter and another chap, a local, judging from his weathered clothes and cloth cap, and whatever he was saying was enough to have them chortling with amusement. In the background she could make out the voice of Roberta Flack, crooning one of her popular love songs. She could only make out snatches of the lyrics because the flow of conversation rolled around the room like the steady rise and fall of surf, punctuated by bursts of laughter.

So far Curtis hadn't spotted her. His back was towards her as he leaned towards his audience, and she took the brief opportunity to rally her forces and get some grim determination into place. She had to weave her way through the tables, and only remembered that they were supposed to be lovers when she was almost on top of them, at which point she forced a smile on her face and just about managed to maintain it when Tom greeted her with a hearty, 'Here's the lucky lass, then! First lady-friend this old rogue has brought to my guest house!'

'Aye, but ye don't know how many he's brought to the house, Tom!' the chap leaning against the counter with them chimed in, at which there was loud, appreciative laughter.

Oh, the wit of men, Jade thought, still wearing the smile.

'Now, now, lads, we don't want to get my beautiful fiancée's imagination working in the wrong direction, do we?' Curtis said, his eyes sweeping over her intimately.

Fiancée? she thought. Isn't that going a bit too far? She tried to incorporate a warning look into the smile which was fast becoming a grimace, but Curtis was having none of it. He slung his arm possessively over her shoulder and nuzzled her ear, squeezing her tightly when her instinct was to leap back in shock.

'Darling, you look ravishing,' he murmured into her hair, and she threw a glassy-eyed and hopefully delighted look at Tom.

'Now, now,' she responded through her teeth, 'let's not overdo it, *darling*.' She prodded him surreptitiously in his ribs, hoping to inflict some pain, but was thwarted by the thickness of his jacket. It turned out to be a poorly thought out manoeuvre, since he promptly gathered the offending hand in his and kissed the flesh of her inner wrist.

The intimate caress wasn't lost on the two men, who gave each other heavy winks and came a bit closer, to witness the scene of romantic cosiness.

After he had released her hand she contained the urge to rub it thoroughly, because oddly it still felt the after-effect of his lips.

'You have a lovely place here, Tom,' Jade said warmly. She edged away from Curtis, only for him to tug her gently back to his side so that she could feel the hard press of his thigh against her body. A gentle, *warning* tug that left her in no doubt that she was required to carry on the charade for as long as was necessary.

'Aye. I have the missus to thank for that, lass. Fancies herself one of them interior designers. Gets samples of wallpapers sent all the time, not a thought in her wee head for the cost!'

'You don't have to think about cost, Tom Hawkins,' Curtis said, smiling. 'I've never known a time when this place wasn't buzzing. Even on a night like this you still manage to draw your regulars. You must put something in the beer that's addictive.'

'Aye, we do all right,' Tom said smugly. He turned to Jade. 'Now, what can I get for the lovely miss?' The other chap levered himself off the bar stool, tilted his cap at her and said that he'd better put his skates on if he wanted to remain in one piece.

'You ladies don't give us a long enough leash,' he complained without rancour. 'Two hours at the pub is all a poor man like myself is allowed.'

'I believe in *very* long leashes, as a matter of fact,' Jade said gaily. 'The less my man is around, the better. Let him have all the space his little heart desires!'

'You know you don't mean that, darling,' Curtis said, with a loving look at her that made her want to pour his drink over his head. 'You can't bear it when I'm not around.' He grinned, enjoying her helpless inability to say anything to the contrary.

'Young love, eh?' Tom poured her a glass of cold white wine and resumed his position at the counter. His teenage son, at the opposite end of the bar, was serving drinks with the expression of someone who could think of a million better things to do.

'Not so young,' Jade replied. 'At least in the case of Curtis…he's quite the old man of the sea!'

'Not so old that I can't appreciate your…womanly qualities.' His hand dropped to her waist and he stroked it, slipping his fingers underneath the jumper so that he could feel bare flesh.

This was taking the game a little too far. She grabbed hold of his wrist, dragged his hand away from its exploration and firmly entwined her fingers with his on the counter.

Tom looked at them warmly.

'Such a nice sight, my young Curtis with a lovely lady like yourself. The missus and I never thought you'd settle down.'

'*Settle down?*' Jade was prepared to deny any such assumption hotly before the net they were building around themselves closed in even tighter. 'I don't think—'

'I know,' Curtis interrupted her with satisfaction. 'I'm pretty amazed by it myself, Tom. I'd given up hope until this…fascinating creature waltzed into my life.'

Fascinating creature? She recalled their first meeting and almost laughed aloud at the memory. 'Fascinating' was hardly one of the descriptions he had hurled at her.

'Love at first sight, was that it?' Tom, engrossed as he was in their fictitious saga, had no qualms about ignoring anyone who wanted to be served. His son, consequently, was rushing around the bar like a bluebottle, pausing only to throw his father ineffectual glares.

'Oh, yes!' Jade beamed. 'Why don't you tell Tom how we met, darling?'

'It's a long story, my friend, but this little minx…' He paused to tenderly push a strand of hair away from her face. The man was a consummate actor, she thought. Oscar-winning, in fact. She fixed him with a beady stare, which resulted in another tender look from him and, sadist that he was, another gentle stroking of hair away from her face. To forestall another such gesture, she briskly and efficiently scraped her hair back and firmly tucked it behind her ears.

'This little minx opened the door to me when I wasn't expected, and mistook me for the plumber!'

Tom looked at her admiringly, as though she had

achieved something very clever with that little stunt. 'You mistook Curtis for a *plumber*?' he asked incredulously.

'I know. A ridiculous mistake. The man wasn't even carrying a tool kit.'

'That must have been a first for you, lad,' Tom said, grinning wickedly and shaking his head.

'That's for sure. First time I've ever been ordered to remove my shoes at the door and pointed in the direction of a leak.'

Tom was still shaking his head with amusement when he handed them the dinner menu. As soon as he had gone, Jade snatched her hand back and said in an undertone, 'What was all *that* in aid of?'

'I told you, my little honey...'

'And you can drop the terms of endearment,' she said drily, 'no one's listening now.'

'I know, but those little terms of endearment seem to *suit* you. Besides, you can never tell. Walls have ears, and we wouldn't want Tom and Rose getting the wrong idea.'

'Don't you mean the *right* idea? And there was no need to elevate me to the status of fiancée. That's going to be a little tricky to undo when you're next up here, isn't it?' She diverted her attention to the menu, turning it over in her hands to inspect the front. There was a childish drawing of a pub, with a crowd of simply sketched people outside, sitting at tables with glasses in their hands.

'Andy's little contribution,' Curtis commented casually. 'He designed it when he was about ten. I used to bring him and Sarah up to the house during their holidays.' When he saw her look of surprise, he raised his eyebrows wryly. 'I gather he never told you?'

'No. I assumed...'

'That I was an ogre. Well, I did take time out, but admittedly I only stayed for a week or so, and the remainder

of the time I flitted up and down and they were left with
the housekeeper and her husband. Andy conveniently for-
gets everything he wants to forget. It's much easier to paint
people in black and white than to realise their nuances.' He
drained the remainder of his beer, then focused his attention
on the list of dishes, leaving her with that little observation
to consider.

Several of the regulars had begun drifting away, not
wanting to tempt fate by staying too late, however close
their homes might be, and by the time they were seated at
one of the tables the place was comfortably empty. Just a
couple by the bar, who seemed more absorbed by what the
weather was doing outside than by each other, and a couple
more who were taking their time with their food.

And the meal, which she had expected to be an agony
of stilted conversation, with her desperately trying not to
focus on what lay ahead, turned out to be a jolly affair,
because both Tom and his wife joined them and within five
minutes she found herself growing more and more intrigued
with all the little snippets of information emerging about
the man sitting opposite her.

The prospect of the roving Curtis Greene settling down
was such a revelation to them that they kept referring to it,
and every time they did Jade shifted uncomfortably in her
chair. He was the sort of man who, faced with a situation
in which fiction was called for, would always fabricate the
most outrageous piece of fiction he could think of, but by
the end of the evening, when their plates had been cleared
away and coffee had been drunk, she was furious with him
for leading these people on. They were so open and charming. How could he? How could he face them next time
with another woman in tow? What phoney excuse would
he use to talk his way out of the impending wedding, the

hat which poor Rose had probably mentally already sorted out?

She was bristling with anger when, at a little after eleven, they made their way to the bedroom.

'You,' she said accusingly, as soon as the bedroom door was firmly shut, 'are a cad. How *could* you maintain that lie about us being engaged? With a smile on your face? Don't you have *any* scruples? How are you going to break it to them when you show up here with some other woman in tow? Tell them that we just weren't suited after all?' She glared at him, and in response he calmly divested himself of his jumper to the shirt underneath. He began to tug it gently out of the waistband of his trousers and she stared at him, aghast. 'And what do you think you're doing?'

'Getting undressed.' He favoured her with a yawn. 'And, no, I won't be using the *we-weren't-suited* excuse. It was clear that they thought we were a match made in heaven.' He grinned, which only enraged her further. Her mind, though, was beginning to stray away from the source of her anger. His shirt was now out of his trousers and he began undoing the buttons on it, very slowly. She watched, open-mouthed and mesmerised, as a sliver of torso was exposed, then all of it as he stripped off the shirt completely and his hand went to the top button of his trousers.

She made a strangled noise and her legs, which wanted to move swiftly in another direction, appeared to be anchored to the square foot of ground underneath them.

She couldn't drag her eyes away from the sight of him, bare-chested, his dark nipples with the swirl of dark hair surrounding them, the rippling lines of his muscles drawing her down to his waist and the arrow of skin that disappeared into the loosened waistband of his trousers. She gulped nervously and licked her lips.

'You're taking your clothes off,' she squeaked stupidly.

'Isn't that what people normally do before they go for a shower?' He unzipped the trousers, and then added as an afterthought, 'Feel free to stand there and watch…'

Her head moved, if not her recalcitrant legs. It swivelled in the direction of the bay window, very firmly averted from the vision standing feet away from her. She heard the sound of his trousers being removed, then the soft thud as they were tossed onto the chair in the corner. He would be standing there, unashamed and naked, or else unashamed and clad only in his underpants. The thought of it brought a film of perspiration over her body and her skin suddenly felt too tight. Then came the padding of his footsteps as he headed towards the bathroom.

'Okay,' he said, with a ring of pure enjoyment in his voice, 'I'm just about to close the door to the bathroom now. As soon as you hear it click, you're safe to move.' She heard the subdued laughter and knew that, whatever he was thinking about her, it certainly didn't involve adjectives such as 'cool', 'sophisticated' or 'worldly wise'.

As soon as she heard the door shut she was galvanised into action. She stripped off, flinging her clothes into the bottom of the wardrobe in an undignified heap, and stuck on her nightie with the speed of light. Then she quickly removed a couple of cushions from the chair, loosely covered them with the top sheet and provided him with one pillow. It was no ideal. There was nothing for him to cover himself with, which meant that he would have to endure an uncomfortably cold sleep, and the makeshift bed was roughly long enough to accommodate a pygmy. His problem, she thought, deciding that removal of make-up and brushing of teeth would have to be abandoned for tonight. He'd got them into this; he would just have to suffer the leg-cramping consequences.

She pulled the duvet up to her chin, switched off the side light and feigned sleep. In fact she was on the point of drifting off when the bathroom door was flung open, and she held her breath, waiting for his reaction to her bed creation. Having initially closed her eyes, she hesitantly opened them to find him still half naked but with drawstring pyjama bottoms on. He was standing in the doorway, and the light framed him so that the shadows playing on the angles of his lithe body made him appear even more powerfully masculine. He was scrutinising the bundle of bedding as though it was something alien that had dropped in from outer space.

'What the hell is that?' he asked, without bothering to move towards it.

'Your sleeping quarters for the night.' Jade yawned widely. Conversation, the gesture said, is now terminated. She rolled onto her side and closed her eyes. She would have preferred to see him well and truly ensconced in his little bed, but on the whole it would be better if she just ignored him completely and let him get on with it. She only released her breath when the bathroom light was switched off, leaving the room in total inky blackness, and she heard him move softly across the room.

Any relief was short-lived.

She heard the sound of bedding, all right, but it was not the sound of bedding being wrapped around six foot two inches of male; it was the sound of bedding hitting her bed. The sheet brushed against her arm and the pillow landed inches from her face, sending her shooting up into a sitting position. She blinked, her eyes adjusting to the darkness, and made out his shadowy hulk following in the wake of the pillow and the sheet. The bed depressed as he climbed in and she clutched the side to stop herself from rolling into contact with him. He prodded the pillow a couple of times, lay down, and she found her voice. At last.

'You were supposed to be sleeping on the floor!' she stuttered in dismay.

'Is *that* what the pillow was doing on the ground!'

'There was a sheet as well,' Jade said through gritted teeth, 'and a couple of cushions.'

'In that case, sorry. I have no intention of sleeping on the ground. Go right ahead if *you* want to, but I wouldn't advise it. When the heating goes off a thin sheet won't go very far to keep the cold out, and I don't particularly want your chattering teeth to rouse me from my beauty sleep.'

With a disgruntled expelling of breath, Jade rolled over onto her other side, making sure that she was safely coccooned. She lay there, her body rigid, attuned to every noise in the room. She could hear the soft swirling of the snow outside. She could also hear his breathing, not quite rhythmic enough to indicate a relaxed state before deep slumber. She knew that there was no way she would get to sleep until she was sure that he was, if she managed to sleep at all.

'Tom and Rose liked you.' His deep, disembodied voice sent a rush of panic through her. This was an abnormal situation, she thought desperately, and reacting in an abnormal manner was just going to make matters worse. She closed her eyes and made deep, regular breathing noises. When he asked whether she was asleep, she breathed a bit more conspicuously, and in the ensuing silence was almost on the verge of thinking that her ploy had succeeded when she felt his hand slide to her waist.

'I *thought* you were still awake,' he said, when she spun around to face him. Bad move. Her face was now inches away from his, and although it was dark in the room it wasn't dark enough to conceal the glitter in his eyes. His

hand was still on her waist, and rather than involve herself
in an undercover tussle to get rid of it, she left it where it
was. When he began to gently caress her side through the
tee shirt, she could feel her treacherous body jerk into life.
The slow, steady flame, which she now realised had been
there for ever, sprang into ferocious life, flooding her with
savage heat that pulsed from the core of her being and
spread outwards, so that her breasts began to ache and her
nipples pushed against the thin jersey.

'Wh…what do you think you're doing…?' she whispered.

'What do you *think* I'm doing?' he whispered back, except, she thought, whereas her whisper had sounded dry
and croaky, his was a velvety, sexy murmur that sent her
pulses racing. 'I'm touching you, Jade,' he expanded, as if
her brain wasn't receiving the message loud and clear.

'You can't.' Since this was not mirrored by any corresponding withdrawal, his stroking hand remained precisely
where it was.

'I won't if you don't want me to, but you do. You want
me to touch you, every part of you, as much as I want it.
Shall I tell you *exactly* what we both want? To explore
each other's bodies. I want to touch you here and…here…'
The roving hand moved inexorably down to her legs, then
up her thigh underneath the tee shirt, where her bare skin
ignited into searing, exciting heat. 'And here…' She
moaned as his fingers skilfully skirted the edge of her
knickers, not seeking to explore but filling her with as much
burning need as if they had. Her body needed this, *craved*
it. Her breathing was coming and going in little gasps.

'I'm turning you on, aren't I? Just watching you turns
me on, do you know that? I thought I'd gone past the point
of fantasising, but ever since I laid eyes on you I've been
fantasising like an adolescent with his first crush.' The soft

murmur of his voice was drawing her deeper and deeper into a vortex of yearning that left her weak and helpless.

Tentatively, she placed the flat of her hand on his chest and felt his indrawn breath. When her hand went lower, to touch his stiff arousal, she felt a sudden surge of heady, erotic power. He was hard and throbbing for her. With a groan, he pushed her onto her back, dislodging the duvet in the process. He caressed her through her tee shirt, massaging her breasts, filling his hands with them, teasing her aching nipples into hard, sensitive protuberances. She wanted him to suckle them so much that it almost physically hurt.

Under his hands, with his mouth wetly laying claim to the white column of her neck, she writhed and twisted.

Her legs parted and she touched herself down there, unable to stand the waiting, and he covered her hand with his, following her movements, then he pushed her hand away and his fingers slid against her wetness. And for a second she very nearly succumbed. She wanted to so badly. But she couldn't. She couldn't, couldn't, couldn't. Her moan of despair so closely resembled a moan of passion that for a split instant he continued to rub her velvety smoothness.

It was only when she curled back that he drew away in surprise.

'I can't.' She tried to keep her voice steady but it was impossible.

'You mean you *won't*, don't you?' His voice was thick with emotion, and she listened to the coolness seeping in with a sinking heart. 'I have more respect for women who say no from the start, Jade. Teasing isn't a feminine ploy I'm into.' The coolness was descending into contempt.

'You don't understand,' she said shakily. 'I want to...but I...I *can't*.'

CHAPTER SEVEN

'WHAT do you mean...*you can't*?' He drew back from her and leaned across the bed to switch on the bedside light. She watched the ripple of his muscles tightening as he inclined his body. Her nerves, which had mysteriously been in suspended animation, clanked into gear, and she could feel perspiration breaking out over her, cooling her down.

'Please switch the light off,' she pleaded. She didn't want to see his face. She didn't want to see his emotions flitting across it. First curiosity, then interest, then the inevitable pulling away as he recognised that he was dealing with someone whose emotional baggage was best left untouched. However complex Curtis Greene was, his attitude to sex would be straightforward. Sex, for him, was fun, and having to deal with someone like her, someone with a story to tell, would not qualify as a fun time. Fun girls didn't weep and cry and pull away. Fun girls laughed and offered nothing beyond simple enjoyment of the moment.

'Why?'

'Because...' Her voice trailed off. 'Because.'

He shrugged and turned the light off, and blessed darkness settled over the room again. She could breathe. He was keeping to his side of the bed now, lazily resting on one elbow. Jade lay flat on her back and stared up at the ceiling.

'I'm listening,' he said, when she showed no inclination to break the silence.

Jade looked across to him and folded her arms on the duvet, across her chest.

'I'm sorry,' she whispered. 'Are you angry with me?'

'Does it make any difference?'

'You *are* angry with me.'

'Just say what you have to say, Jade.'

Oh, God. Was that boredom in his voice? Did he think that she was going to make up a string of lies because basically she had exercised her woman's prerogative to say no at the last minute? Did he think that she was that kind of girl? She wondered *what* kind of girl she was, and realised that she no longer knew. She had been in mourning for over two years, and now, when she should tentatively be feeling her way towards a relationship, she had jumped straight into bed with a man with whom a relationship was out of the question. It made no sense, and even before everything had happened she had always been a sensible girl.

'I have a problem…' she began. *Once upon a time,* she should have started. *Once upon a time, there were two happy little girls.* Her hands were beginning to feel clammy. This was the first time that she was ever going to talk about this, about how she felt, about how her life had been eaten away, leaving her incapable of facing the future. 'I've been in counselling.'

'Is it drugs?'

'No, of course it's not drugs! The only drugs I've ever taken have been paracetamol for the occasional headache.' She laughed, and felt a little better for it. 'I…I wish I knew where to begin…' She sighed and thought of her sister, a rapid mental recall that spanned all the years of her childhood and adolescence, into her twenties. 'I had a twin…Caroline…' Just saying the name out loud brought a lump to her throat.

'Take your time,' he said gently, and she threw him a watery smile, not sure whether he could make it out clearly or not.

'We were very close...'

'*Were?*'

'She died a little over two years ago...' She waited for him to interrupt with some polite lip service to sympathy, and when he didn't say anything she drew in a deep breath. 'We were very close. Incredibly close. We were brought up single-handedly by our mum, and when we were seventeen Mum died and we were left to fend for ourselves.'

She smiled to herself as she remembered how their mother's death had brought their very different personalities into stark relief. Jade, always the more responsible of the two, had assumed the mantle of authority and Caroline had automatically turned to her for support. In the space of a few months they had developed into a clear older and younger sister relationship, even though they'd been the same age. She had been the one to make sure that there was a meal in the evening, that the washing got done, that the schoolwork got done, and even when she had carried on studying and Caroline had quit school to get a job she had still continued to run the household alongside her own work.

'I take it from your tone of voice that you were the one to do most of the fending?' he said shrewdly. He stroked the side of her face, rubbing the pad of his thumb against her cheekbone, and instead of retreating into her defensiveness she found that she enjoyed the fleeting touch.

'It worked well for the both of us,' Jade said matter-of-factly.

'And then what happened?'

'Things were going very nicely for a while,' Jade said. Her face felt damp but she wasn't quite sure why. She didn't think that she had been crying, but she supposed she must have been. Crying in a quiet, leaky kind of way, the sort of crying that can go on for a lifetime. 'Years, in fact.

I finished my A levels, then I started doing an art course at university. Caroline's job was going well, although she was always one to party away the rungs on the career ladder. She liked going out. She was beautiful, beautiful and sexy, and she liked the attention that her looks brought her.

'I can remember boys calling for her when we were thirteen and I still thought that boys were irritating little creatures who got in the way of study. Caroline's idea of study was to open textbooks about two weeks before an exam and then try to force-feed the information into her brain. I can ever remember her going to sleep with a maths book underneath her pillow because someone had told her that she would absorb the information better that way!' She laughed, and hiccoughed, and when he handed her a handkerchief, produced from where she had no idea, she took it and dabbed her face.

This wasn't as hard as she had thought it was going to be. She had thought that she might not be able to get past the first mention of her sister's name, but now, in full flow, she found that reliving the memories was not as painful as anticipated.

'And where did *you* fit in to this scenario?' he asked softly. Her eyes had long acclimatised to the darkness. She could make out the softened angles of his face and the sympathetic expression in his eyes.

'I enjoyed my sister's antics from the sidelines. It probably sounds weird, but just watching the array of men she brought home was enough to leave me feeling exhausted.'

'You must have had your own array as well...'

Jade shook her head. 'Far from it. I was hell-bent on finishing my art course. Men were something I sort of assumed would crop up when I had more time on my hands. There were one or two boyfriends, of course, but nothing...you know, out of the ordinary.' The words were com-

ing out of her so fluently that she could hardly believe that
it was she talking. Opening up to another human being had
never felt so easy.

'Nothing out of the ordinary...' he half murmured.

No, she thought, *not like you.* The simplicity of the real-
isation shocked her into sudden silence. Curtis Greene was
an extraordinary man who had done something extraordinary to her.

'Carry on with your story,' he said softly. 'Finish the tale
you began.'

'So that your curiosity can be satisfied?'

She saw him frown. 'Is that why you think I'm listening?
Because I'm curious? Do you think that once my curiosity
is sated I'll roll over to my side of the bed and go to sleep?'

'I remember you saying that you liked the challenge of
a mystery.'

'Stop it, Jade.'

'Stop what?'

'Trying to run away and hide behind words. Stop trying
to turn me into a bastard to protect yourself.'

'I'm not,' she protested heatedly, thinking that he had
hit the nail on the head. 'Okay. I'll finish. I want to anyway.
I owe it to you.'

'You don't owe me anything. You don't owe me any
explanations for your behaviour. If you want to talk about
this, then do it because you *want* to, not because you think
you should.'

'Caroline started getting...these attacks of breathless-
ness. She'd be fine, then suddenly she'd have to sit down.
At first we both thought that it was because she'd been
burning the candle at both ends. But it didn't get any better,
even after she'd stopped some of her partying and started
trying to get a few good nights' sleep. So...so she went to
the doctor.'

Jade lay back. She could feel her fingers gripping into the flesh of her upper arms and she forced herself to keep her voice neutral.

'They did a lot of tests on her and finally they broke the news. She had a congenital heart defect. Not one of those that kill without warning, but it wasn't curable. She still had time left, but not much. And after that everything changed. The life went out of her, even though she tried to keep up a brave face. I quit my art course. I had very nearly reached the end of it, but I felt that I should start earning money, just to make the remainder of her life easier. We went on a couple of holidays and I spent all that time with her, building up to the inevitable. Except when the inevitable came, it found me as unprepared as if I'd never known it was going to happen.'

She turned her head to look at him. 'I fell apart. Not a great big falling apart. More a steady unravelling from all the seams. I moved to London, got a job, but basically my life had stopped. I couldn't face doing anything, seeing anyone. All I could think was that if it had happened to her, then it should have happened to me as well. We were twins. How could our bodies have had such a crucial difference between them?'

She looked at him pleadingly, willing for him to give her some kind of meaningful answer. He looked as though he had taken a body blow and was literally unable to speak. When he finally did, his voice was rough and unsteady.

'Nothing I can say can make sense of what you've just told me,' he said. 'How can it? If we could work out the reasons behind all the brutal, unfair things that happen in life, then we'd hold the key to the universe in our hands. All we can do is work with what we've been dealt. All I can tell you is that I'm sorry.'

'I'm getting better.' She wasn't blubbing, but her eyes

still hurt like hell. She felt better, though, better than she had felt in a long time. 'I went to see a counsellor and that was a turning point for me. Just to be able to talk about it. That's when I decided to take back up the art. That's when I met your brother.'

'At counselling?' There was bewilderment in his voice. 'You met Andy at a counselling session?'

'More than one, actually. It was a sort of trial, group thing. We hit it off from the start. He made me laugh and he was my shoulder to cry on.'

'Why was he there?'

'Why do you think? His own personal stresses were getting too much for him. We encouraged one another.'

'Don't go on,' Curtis told her, with a hint of urgency in his voice. 'I'm beginning to get jealous.' He tempered the statement with a laugh, and the passing thought that he might really have been jealous was immediately squashed. 'Is that why you can't...touch me? Why you don't feel comfortable with the opposite sex?'

She wanted to tell him that she normally felt quite comfortable with the opposite sex, just so long as they remained at an arm's length away, then realised that he had unsettled her on all fronts from the start. He had certainly made her feel alive. For the first time she had begun to see the truth behind what people said, all those old clichés about dear ones being gone but that doesn't mean that you are as well. He would never know it, but he had dragged her kicking and screaming, figuratively, into being a responsive, living, breathing, whole human being again.

'I...yes...can you begin to understand?'

Instead of answering, he leaned forward and planted a brotherly kiss on her forehead.

'Goodnight, Jade. Sweet dreams.' He rolled onto his side, and for a few seconds she decided that she was so relieved that it had all been settled in such an amicable fashion. She had been truthful with him and there were no misunderstandings now to clutter their relationship. If what they had could be classed as a relationship.

He would stop flirting with her because he would know that she was no longer available, in any way, shape or form. That brotherly peck on the forehead was indication enough of that. He would treat her like a piece of china, respect her need for privacy, not try and needle her into any more heated outpourings. She had sorted out her own mystery for him, and now that he understood she knew that he would cease all attempts to seduce her with his personality. If he had ever been trying to seduce her.

Not that she wanted to be seduced.

She stared at the broad back. Above the duvet, she could see the top of his spine and the hard ridges of his shoulders. His head, inclined forward towards his chest, showed the vulnerable nape of his neck. She stared so hard at it that her eyes began to burn. He was asleep. She was sure that he was. His breathing was very regular. No twitchy movements. She waited for a few more minutes. If her eyes were lasers, she would surely have burnt a hole into his neck by now. A neat little hole just there, where his black hair tapered into a V shape.

She reached out and touched the spot. It was enough. Enough to send every nerve-ending in her body into overdrive. The touch became a gentle stroke with the knuckles of her fingers and she felt his body still.

She wanted him so badly that she thought she was imagining his response when his hand caught her fingers and one by one he put each finger into his mouth, sucking and licking them.

No dream.

She moaned softly and he turned to face her. 'Do you want this?' he asked huskily.

'I'm not that kind of girl.' Not the kind of girl who lets her hands roam feverishly over a man's body, touching his nipples, feeling the flat, hard planes of his stomach, pushing down the loose elasticated waistband of his silk pyjamas so that she could feel, caress, stroke.

'Not *what* kind of girl? The kind of girl who wants to feel alive again?' His voice was unsteady as she began edging closer to him, with his powerful arousal still firmly in her hand. Closer so that she could lift her tee shirt and grind her hips against his, loving the feel of him against her through her underwear.

She couldn't recall what kind of girl she was supposed to be. She just knew that right here and right now she was *this* type, and if that meant that she wanted to feel alive again, then so be it.

Her breasts, pinioned under her arm, felt swollen and heavy. She had to get her tee shirt off. She was burning up.

She sat up, and with one swift movement pulled it over her head. Before she could lie back down on her side, he had hoisted himself up enough to hold one of her swinging breasts in his hand, then he leant forward and began licking it. His tongue flicked over the soft swell, traced beneath it, teasing her mercilessly, so that when he finally absorbed her nipple into his mouth she groaned with satisfaction.

'Oh, yes, oh, yes, oh, yes.' She curled her fingers into his hair and flung back her head. She never wanted this to stop and, as if sensing her need, he levered her onto her back, pinning her hands with his while he continued to lick and suck her nipples. She felt them hard in his mouth, and when he nipped the protuberances gently with his teeth she began to writhe with mounting passion.

'What do you want me to do to you?' he asked, moving his hips against hers. He pulled off his pyjama bottoms, then her underwear, and supported himself above her, letting her feel him, taking her to dizzy heights but resisting the final thrust.

'Anything,' she half sobbed, 'but just don't stop.'

This was a different body. A new body with heightened responses and no inhibition. She opened herself to him in a way that she had never done to anyone in her life before, and, limited though her sexual experience was, she knew that this had nothing to do with the fact that she was emerging from her emotional deep freeze. This was unique to this particular man. Curtis Greene had somehow unlocked her, and she revelled in it.

Her passion was only matched by his. His muttered crudities, which would have been like a bucket of cold water had they come from anyone else, were deliciously sexy when he spoke them, in a rough, unsteady voice. He was aggressive, but with an expertise that left her wanting more, and his aggression fired her own wanton abandon.

When his mouth found her most intimate place, she pushed his head still closer against her, gyrating her hips with circular movements that resembled a dance, arching her body back so that she could savour the licking of his tongue.

How was it that she had never felt like this before? He touched and explored every inch of her willing body and she found that she was doing the same to him.

When neither of them could stem the oncoming flood of release, he moved over her and filled her with his manhood. If a tornado had hit the guest house, she doubted whether either of them would have been aware of it.

She only became aware of the silence in the room, which

had echoed to the sound of their passion, when they were finally lying next to one another, spent.

It had all seemed so natural, so *right*, that she felt not the slightest twinge of regret, even though she knew that there was plenty of that waiting in the wings for her.

'You,' he said huskily, cupping her bottom with his hands so that there was barely an inch of space between their damp bodies, 'are beautiful. Spectacular.'

'Beautiful? Spectacular?' she teased, stroking his cheek with her finger. 'That has the ring of a cliché about it. Is it what you tell all those willing women whom you lure into bed with you?'

'I don't do *lure*,' he murmured, 'and I don't do *women*. I'm very discriminating when it comes to the fair sex, and you, my darling, are the fairest of them all.'

Darling? She wasn't sure whether she had heard right. Had he just called her *darling*? Did it mean anything? She fought against getting lost in analysis of an endearment which had been muttered in the pleasant afterglow of lovemaking.

'Do you still object to sharing the bed with me now?' he asked with teasing gravity.

Jade wanted to tell him that she would object to *not* sharing the bed with him, but caution, dreary though it seemed, was not to be tossed to the four winds. She wanted him, and there was no point in trying to disguise the fact or apologise for it, but some inner voice of common sense warned her against betraying too much of her feelings.

She went to sleep after more lazy lovemaking that was just as satisfactory, holding the memory of that endearment close to her heart, and awoke to a view of leaden skies and snow streaming down. Curtis was standing by the window looking out, and to her intense delight he didn't have a stitch of clothing on. She had a few seconds of pure, undiluted enjoyment of the sight before he turned around and smiled at her.

'You're awake, Sleeping Beauty.'

Jade stretched and yawned. 'It's still snowing.'

'All the more excuse for us to keep each other warm.' He began walking slowly towards the bed and she followed him with her eyes, provocatively pulling the duvet down so that her breasts were exposed. He paused at the foot of the bed, and the intensity of his look was as much of a turn-on as if he had reached out and touched her. A turn-on, she thought with some satisfaction, for the both of them, judging from the way his body was reacting to the sight.

With a sinful lack of inhibition she began to roll her fingers over her nipples, teasing them into full erection, enjoying this sexual lovemaking that was visual only. The anticipation of what lay ahead was enough to send waves of desire surging through her.

The room was beautifully warm and she languidly kicked off the duvet, so that the rest of her nudity was on show, and very slowly trailed one hand along her stomach, then to the soft curls between her thighs. She watched as a slow smile crossed his face, but he waited until she had touched herself into mounting passion before he swiftly joined her on the bed and, with exquisite lack of haste, completed the job she had begun.

By the time they finally left the pleasurable warmth of the bed it was nearly nine-thirty, and downstairs Tom was already up and busy.

The indulgent, knowing look he shot them as they strolled towards him brought a faint pink flush to her cheeks.

'How did you two sleep?' he asked, interrupting himself to shout to Rose, who was somewhere behind the area of the bar, that Curtis and the wee lass would be ready for some breakfast.

'Oh, there wasn't much of that, Tom,' Curtis said, raising his hand to roughly caress the nape of her neck beneath her hair. 'But the fault didn't lie with the mattress.'

'Say no more, son.' His grin grew broader, as did the pinkness in Jade's cheeks.

This was heavenly. This warm, possessive tenderness that Curtis was showing towards her. He made her feel special and desirable, and she intended to bask in the sensation for as long as the snow continued falling. It would end, because all things did, but there was no law against enjoying it while it lasted.

'What d'ye make of our fine Scottish weather, lassie?' asked Tom, showing them to the very same table they had sat at the night before.

'I always knew that it never stopped snowing in Scotland,' Jade answered gravely. 'I bet it even does this in the summer time.'

'Aye, it takes its time giving in to spring,' he replied with the same mock gravity. 'When we're all heartily fed up with its winter antics.'

'Doesn't look like it intends to give in at the moment,' Curtis remarked, with something approaching satisfaction in his voice. He was speaking to Tom, but his eyes were on Jade, and she had the same feeling of being touched even though that wasn't the case.

'Not for another day or two,' Tom told them thoughtfully, glancing over his shoulder, then heading towards the kitchen.

'Well, I guess we'll just have to find things to do to occupy ourselves, won't we?' Curtis shot her a wicked, teasing look, and she entered into the game, shaking her head with a puzzled frown.

'Are there any places of interest around here?' she asked. 'Accessible by foot?'

'Oh, I can certainly think of one place of interest,' he said softly, leaning towards her across the small rectangular table, 'accessible by hand.'

He watched with gratification as a schoolgirl blush spread across her cheeks.

'I love to see you blush like that,' he murmured, reaching out and caressing the side of her face, as though he couldn't help himself. 'Hasn't anyone ever made love to you with words before?'

'Not…not that I can remember,' Jade replied breathlessly, dropping her eyes.

'Well, now, here's the perfect opportunity for me to put that right.'

The perfect opportunity had to be relinquished in favour of breakfast, as Rose bustled in with two enormous plates of eggs, bacon, oatcakes, baked beans and steaming mugs of coffee.

'I shall get fat,' said Jade, tucking into the food with gusto. 'If I have two more days of hearty Scottish fare, I won't be able to waddle out of the door.'

'Bit of an exaggeration, but never fear. If it comes to that, we can always arrange some kind of pulley system for you through the window. Or else we can just stay put here for as long as it takes for you to go on a diet and lose the weight.'

'Oh, dear, I wouldn't dream of having you miss work.'

'When it comes to your very…edible body, it wouldn't be too much of a sacrifice, I assure you.'

The word *edible* reminded her of just how tasty he had found her body the evening before, and she hurriedly concentrated on her food and heard him chuckle under his breath.

This was sheer madness, but for the first time since her sister's illness had been diagnosed Jade felt wonderfully free. She knew that sooner or later one of them would have to mention the inevitable subject of what would happen when they returned to London. She also knew that before she was forced to hear him say that London was reality, as opposed to Scotland, which was a bit of unexpected fun, she would say it herself first. She would retreat with dignity, and just in case the dignity proved to be skin-deep she would leave the shared house and find alternative lodgings. The prospect of that was such a blight on the horizon that she pushed it to one side. What was the point of crossing the bridge before you came to it?

And here, in this snow-covered wilderness, it was easy to forget about tomorrow.

She discovered just how easy when they went for a walk and she found herself doing things she hadn't done since she was a child, and then only infrequently, because snow was something that had only ever flirted lightly with her home town.

She had certainly never made a six-foot-tall snowman in her life before; that much she could state with absolute certainty.

They worked away at it for an hour and a half, until they no longer felt the biting cold through their layers of clothing, and at the end of their mammoth task she stood back, surveyed their creation and said wonderingly, 'It looks just like you.'

'In which case we must bear an uncanny resemblance to one another, because I was about to say the same thing about you!' He grinned at her and she made a snowball, packing it tightly in her gloved hands, and struck home.

The only problem with escape was that it was impossible to run in inches of snow, and she was laughing gleefully when he pulled her down and kissed her very thoroughly before allowing her back to her feet.

'Naughty little girls must be punished,' he informed her, in his best school teacher voice, which naturally propelled her into a full-frontal attack and a fully declared cold war.

'Peace!' she said, holding up her hands when she had been splattered with enough snowballs to construct another six-foot snowman.

'Are you admitting defeat?'

'I am.'

'In which case,' he said, with a theatrical bow, 'I generously accept my role of victor. In which case, I get to choose the spoils...' Jade folded her arms, grinning, and he chucked her under the chin. 'An amble in the direction of the house.'

'You said yesterday that walking to the house was out of the question!'

'Oh, I shouldn't think we'll make it there. In fact, I *know* we won't, but you might be able to catch a glimpse of it.'

'That big, is it? Those wings'll do it every time, won't they?'

Will the real Curtis Greene please stand up? she thought, as they walked as far as they could go, which wasn't very far, and he regaled her with stories of New York, making her laugh with his anecdotes, getting her to regale him with a few of her own and gently helping her over the obstacle of her sister's death.

The words seemed to have accumulated inside her and were bursting now to be freed. She remembered amusing incidents that she had thought forgotten, and the more they spoke, the more she felt the weave of the net surrounding her tighten.

This felt so good and so real, but it was merely an illusion. Like all illusions, though, she was powerless to fight it. As powerless to fight the inroads he was making into her soul as she was to fight the responses of her body when he touched it.

And he was almost boyishly pleased at all the firsts he was providing for her.

A first, he said later that evening, counting them out on his fingers, for building a six-foot snowman.

A first for eating haggis, which he assured her was perfectly delicious when you forgot what went into it.

And a first for being engaged; he grinned rakishly when she opened her mouth to dispute that one.

Two days later, with the snow finally beginning to show signs of abating, she realised that there were an awful lot more she could add to his categories.

Curtis Greene was a first when it came to showing her just how fulfilling lovemaking could be. In between the teasing, the conversation and the companionable silences, they had made love with the urgency of two people who knew that time and reality were not on their side. Until him, she had never shared a shower with a man before, and had never even contemplated that the simple act of getting clean could become an erotic exploration of bodies.

Until him, she had never revealed herself to anyone. She had scattered confidences around here and there, things that were of no real significance, but with him she had laid bare her soul, never mind the consequences.

It was only when they had packed their bags, three days after they had first arrived, and the prospect of London was looming on the horizon like a black cloud heavy with foreboding, that the elusive thought that had been nibbling away at the back of her mind took shape and revealed itself.

Curtis Greene had proved himself a first in the most disastrous way.

He was the first man she had ever fallen in love with,

and she knew, with a sinking, wretched feeling, that he would be the last.

Through all their discussions by day and pillow-talk by night not once had the word *love* ever crossed his lips.

Wanting, yearning, craving…that was the vocabulary of lust. And lust was nothing more than water through your fingers. For a while, you could capture it, but sooner rather than later it trickled away, never to reappear.

As they waved goodbye to Tom and she played out the final charade of impending marriage with a hollow emptiness in the pit of her stomach, she knew that before the snow had melted from the car she would be gone.

CHAPTER EIGHT

THE snow was passable, but still thick enough to make driving a lengthy business, and now that Jade had made up her mind that she was leaving the house her attitude altered as the city grew nearer.

She thought that Curtis hadn't noticed, after all his concentration was fixed heavily on the road, but as soon as the drive became smoother he said, without looking at her, 'Are you going to tell me?'

'Tell you what?' She jumped at the abruptness of the question, and when she looked at his profile it was to find him staring directly ahead, his face grim and unsmiling. Miserably she thought that he was feeling what she was as well. The tug of reality was banishing those few days in their wilderness, turning it into a hazy dream, misting over the sharp edges. By the time they were on the plane his mind would be racing ahead to work, and the humorous, sexy man she had found and fallen in love with would become a disturbing stranger in whose life she no longer had a role.

'Tell me why you've suddenly turned into a block of ice.' He risked taking his eyes off the road for a split second to look at her. 'What's the matter? Aren't you pleased to be leaving our enforced state of isolation?' He offered a hair's breadth of a pause, into which she steadfastly refused to drop any kind of answer.

Was that how he viewed their time together? As enforced isolation. So what the hell? Might as well make the most of it by getting into bed with the woman who happened to find herself alongside him? It hadn't seemed that way back there, but hadn't she seen for herself just how consummate an actor the man was?

'Of course I'm pleased,' Jade replied neutrally, turning her head to stare out of the window. In a short while they would be at the airport and she could feign sleep on the flight.

'You don't look pleased,' he mused, giving her more of his undivided attention now that he no longer had to focus single-mindedly on the road. 'You should be smiling, whistling a merry tune…maybe you miss our enforced isolation…? I know what's going through your head,' he murmured roughly, 'but there's no need for this to end…'

'What do you mean?' Jade's heart began to gallop. Don't be ridiculous, she told herself, and the thought was promptly and absurdly followed by a series of sharp mental clips of the two of them, growing old together, blissfully married, children pattering about. In winter an open fire, a cosy sofa, and maybe bedroom slippers, or was that a little fuddy-duddy? The galloping heart turned into a fast trot. In a minute it would be racing. This was what she wanted. She wanted Curtis Greene for ever and beyond. She wanted to go to bed with him at night and arise with him in the morning. She wanted to go shopping with him, cook meals with him and share every nuance of her life with him. Stupid, stupid, stupid.

'I mean,' he said, glancing across at her, 'exactly what I said. There's no need for this to come to an end. Because we're heading back to London doesn't mean that we have to pretend that nothing happened between us. Let's face it, Jade, there's something between us, some kind of chemistry, and it's been there from the very moment we first laid eyes on one another. At least for me. The past few days have been good. No, more than good. Spectacular.'

His voice swam around her in velvety waves and she sank a little lower into the seat. Shame that the airport was getting closer and closer. This was what she wanted to hear. It was music to her ears. She only wished that she had a portable tape recorder with her so that she could record it all and play it back over and over again.

'Yes, it's been…good. Very good,' she answered dreamily. She slanted her head to look at him, absorbing every inch of his face lovingly.

'So you agree with me, then, do you? That there's no point fighting it? Do you know,' he added softly, his mouth curving into a smile that sent shivers of pleasure racing through her, 'even when we were at each other's throats, I still felt a crazy urge to get my hands on you? I still wanted to rip your clothes off and take all that fighting to bed, see for myself whether all that fire was just on the outside.'

There was a certain masculine smugness in his voice that thrilled her. She wondered what kind of father he would make. A good one, she suspected, ferociously devoted. A brilliant father to their two children. Or maybe four—Caroline's premature death had cruelly brought home to her the fact that she was now an orphan, and it was a fate she would wish on no one.

'You're already living in my house,' he continued, while her mind carried on playing with glorious fantasies of miniature Curtis Greenes scampering about the grand house, felt-tip pens in hands, wreaking marvellous chaos on the impeccable furnishings. 'You would just need to change rooms.'

She was so wrapped up in her cosy little dreams that it took a second or two for what he said to sink in.

'Change rooms…?'

'Well, it *would* be more convenient if we were to conduct

an affair, wouldn't it? Andy's a big boy now. I don't think he'll have a problem coping with us sharing a bed.'

'And how long would this…change of rooms…last?' Jade asked faintly. The wonderfully racing heart was turning into the dull pounding of drums, the type of drums designed for everlasting headaches, the type of drums that brought on nausea and panic.

'For the duration.'

'For the duration. Of course.' She bit her upper lip and tucked her hands into the pockets of her coat, balling them into clenched fists.

For the duration. That said it all. The duration could be a month, six months, maybe even a year, but it would never be permanent. There would be no domestic bliss and the patter of tiny feet. In their place would be the sweaty grinding of bodies at night until his desire faded, at which point he would politely remind her that he had never promised permanence. If he still had any feelings left, he would undoubtedly give her time to find herself somewhere to live.

She thought of her mother, her sister. The people she loved all disappeared. What was she doing? What had she done? Given away yet more love so that what…? She could indulge it for a few weeks, secure in the knowledge that at the end of that time she would have to cope with yet more hurt?

'You wouldn't even have to think about money,' he said, filling in the silent gaps. 'You could do your art course without having to scrimp and save. I would make sure that you had everything you wanted.'

Jade didn't say anything. She turned away and gazed out of the window. Love wasn't supposed to be like this. She knew that it was never plain, calm sailing, but neither was it about buying, because wasn't that what he was offering her? Comfort, luxury, even, because as his mistress she knew that her every material wish would be indulged, but in exchange for sex. Oh, she could go with this tide and hope that his caring would one day turn into something less disposable, but the thought was stillborn.

'Is that what they call a "modern relationship"?' she enquired dully. 'Man meets woman, man lusts after woman, man toys around with her for a while, then man disposes of her?'

His grip on the steering wheel tightened.

'That's over-simplifying it, and anyway, there's nothing to say that *you* won't be the one to walk away.'

'Is it?' She gazed briefly out of the window, then turned to look at him. 'You're asking me to sleep with you in return for your largesse. But of course it will end, and then what? Do I return everything you've given me, meekly pack my suitcase and find myself some rented accommodation?'

'I'm not saying anything of the sort!' he exploded harshly.

'Then what *are* you saying? Please clarify, because it seems that I'm too thick to understand.'

'You're not too thick to understand. You're *deliberately* misunderstanding. You're reducing it all to some kind of financial bargaining, which couldn't be further from what I have in mind. If you feel insulted by my offer to help you out financially then that's not a necessity. It may not occur to you that I might actually *like* the thought of spending money on you, of indulging your every whim.'

For how long? she thought restlessly. Her novelty value would no doubt kindle generous, magnanimous feelings in him, but a novelty by its own definition was something with a limited timespan.

Without her realising it, they were nearing the airport,

and she breathed a sigh of relief that their conversation would come to an end.

'What will you do about the car?'

'What…are you talking about?' As he drove slowly into the airport car park he turned to look at her, as though she was completely mad.

'The car. What are you going to do? Is someone going to come and collect it?'

'I'm trying to have a serious conversation with you and you're talking about *the fate of the bloody car*?' He banged his fist against the wheel and then, spotting a space, screeched into it with a reckless lack of caution. His face was grim as he yanked their cases out of the boot of the car and slammed down the bonnet.

'The car,' he grated, 'will have a pleasant little overnight stay here and then will be collected tomorrow morning. I shall phone my chap and tell him where exactly it is. All niggling questions on that front satisfied?' He began striding towards the airport while Jade trailed behind him.

'I just wondered,' she said breathlessly, trying to match his long strides and avoid colliding with other people at the same time.

'So what you're telling me,' he said in an infuriatingly patient tone of voice that was not lost on the girl behind the counter taking their tickets, 'is that it's okay to sleep with me for a few days because we happened to find ourselves confined by snow to a guesthouse with only one spare room, but that it's somehow *not* okay to carry on sleeping together when we get back to London. What kind of weird, twisted morality do you call that?'

Jade furiously mouthed at him to keep his voice down. The girl staring down at the tickets and punching numbers into the computer in front of her was fighting to hide a grin.

'Sorry? I can't hear you. Were you trying to answer my question? You'll have to speak up. I'm not a lip-reader.'

Professional etiquette was struggling hard against an inclination to laugh, and Jade looked meaningfully at the girl's downturned head, then glared a warning at Curtis.

'Oh, *I* understand. You *will* excuse us having a personal discussion, won't you?' he said to the girl in a silky voice, and she met his blue eyes with a broad smile.

'Please carry on. You'd be amazed at some of the things I hear at this counter.' She carried on with what she was doing while Jade simmered in stubborn silence.

'We were discussing your dubious morality,' he said.

'*You* were discussing my dubious morality,' she hissed back. '*I* wasn't discussing anything of the sort, because this is neither the time nor the place...' She had lowered her voice so that it was practically inaudible. If he told her to speak up again, then she would clout him, whatever the captive audience. He had just turned her world on its head, and the worst of it was that he couldn't understand.

He thought that it was a simple matter of two people who fancied each other hopping into bed for glorious sex with no strings attached. She, on the other hand, wanted to scream that glorious sex would only be glorious sex if there were thousands of strings attached, and the thought of having such antiquated, laughable Victorian notions in this day and age of fast living and casual love was enough to make her cringe. How would *he* respond? With incredulity? Guffaws of laughter? Cold sweats and horror?

The ginger-haired girl handed him back his ticket and went through the routine explanation of which gate to go to and what time the plane would be leaving.

'Hope you sort your differences out,' she added with a hesitant smile, and relaxed when Curtis afforded her one of his earth-shattering ones in return.

'I'm sure we will.'

Over my dead body, Jade thought darkly.

'So,' he said conversationally, as they walked towards the departure gate, 'shall we continue what we were talking about, or perhaps you have some other urgent and totally inconsequential subject you'd like to raise?'

'I don't intend to become your mistress,' she answered briefly. 'Is that so hard for you to accept?'

'It is when you stop to consider what we've spent the last few days doing.'

'Will you stop reminding me of that?'

'Why? Does it make you uncomfortable to think that you've slept with me, wherever and whenever and with an admirable lack of restraint, yet here you are now, mouthing a lot of principles and playing the outraged virgin? Talk about trying to lock the stable door after the horse has bolted.' He laughed harshly.

'I'm not denying that…that we slept together…'

'That's very clear-sighted of you! But it was simply an aberration, is that it? Brought on by the extreme weather conditions?'

'Yes, it was an aberration, just a bit of fun…'

'You used me, didn't you?' His eyes narrowed ominously. Thank heavens he was not conducting this conversation in the same elevated tones he had used earlier on. From the look on his face, she suspected that bystanders would find what he was about to say very intriguing indeed.

She looked at him warily. 'Used you for what?'

'As a form of therapy. You yourself admitted that your sister's death catapulted you into a physical deep freeze. Was I your method of thawing out, Jade?' His voice was no longer a whiplash, but his eyes on her were still curious and hard. Just the thought of being used, for whatever reason, would be enough to bring all debate on the subject to a complete stop, and although that was the result she wanted, a lie was not the route she cared to take to get there.

'No,' she admitted reluctantly. They had arrived for their flight with no time to spare and she followed as they boarded the plane and took their seats in the first class section.

She couldn't quite believe that they were still having this conversation. He had made a proposition, she had declined, what more was there to say? He must have suffered a tremendous blow to his masculine pride, she decided, if he couldn't let the matter rest. But the longer he nibbled away at the edges of her resolve, the less certain she felt about the decision she had taken. Her arguments for not sleeping with him made no logical sense, yet she couldn't expose her feelings, so she was left floundering in a limbo of incomprehensible mumbo-jumbo and self-justification.

'Then *what* is the problem?' he demanded, exasperated.

'The problem is that I'm not ready to climb into any sort of relationship, even a relationship of a temporary nature. What happened back there seemed…right, but I don't intend to stretch it out. I'd prefer to leave it as a pleasant memory.'

'*A pleasant memory?* We're not talking about a ramble through the countryside! And you don't have to view this as a potential relationship. You could just see it as a thoroughly satisfying fling between two people who are attracted to one another. No strings attached.'

'So you already said. I don't want to talk about this any more,' Jade said, retreating into mutinous silence. Every word he spoke was like a knife being twisted deeper into an already open wound. In a minute he would get a tub of table salt and compound the pain by rubbing the lot in, and she was not going to give him the chance of doing that. 'When we get back, I'm going to pack up and go.'

'Don't be bloody childish. If you do that you'll be cutting off your nose to spite your face. Have you even got anywhere you could run to? A friend's floor somewhere?' When she didn't answer he nodded, as though he understood what she was trying not to say. 'As I suspected. Nowhere to run. Why play the martyr, Jade? I'm not telling you that you have to leave the house just because you don't want to sleep with me.'

'I know you're not. I just think that it would be all-round easier if...'

'Easier for *you*, you mean. Because if you're not around me, then you need never face the risk of having your self-control slip a little, need you? Or maybe you're scared that *I* might find myself banging on your bedroom door to get in. You needn't worry, Jade. I've never crawled for a woman in my life before, and I don't intend to start now.'

'I never said that!' The man sitting across the aisle from them glanced across in their direction and she lowered her voice. 'Now can we let the matter rest?'

'More fool you,' he muttered, or else something along those lines.

'Why? Because you think that you're God's gift to womankind and I'd be an idiot to throw away a few more weeks of your attention? Before you move on?'

Dawning comprehension stole across his face and he gazed at her as if seeing her for the first time. 'So *that's* what it's all about,' he said slowly. 'You think that I intend to pick you up and toss you aside when I'm done with you...'

'I'm not saying anything of the sort. I'm just saying that... I don't want involvement... I'm not talking about…you know… I want to concentrate on my work…I don't want to have any distractions…'

'You don't want a fling, do you?' he mused. 'You want the full works. Marriage, ring on finger, commitment…that's what this is all about, isn't it?'

'Of course not!'

The man across from them looked up, shifted a bit in the seat and settled back to his newspaper, but she could tell from his body language that he was all ears.

'Of course not,' she muttered. 'I can't think of anything worse than marriage. Ha! I'm now setting off on my life or so it seems. Do you imagine that I want to clutter it up with anything like *commitment*? Does that make sense to you?'

'No, but it makes more sense than the rubbish you've been coming out with so far.'

'You,' she fulminated, 'are egotistic, bull-headed, arrogant and infuriating.'

'Actually, I prefer to think of myself as quietly charming, incredibly intelligent, devilishly amusing and, generally speaking, a fount of most wisdom.' He relaxed back in the chair, folded his arms and closed his eyes.

Why was he looking so damned satisfied? she wondered.

'The mere fact that you can trot out all that stuff shows that you're egotistic and infuriating!'

The newspaper had been abandoned by the man sitting opposite them. He was now feigning a light doze, as was Curtis, who was now also wearing a ghost of a smile on his face. It was *highly irritating*.

'And what are you *smiling about* anyway?' she ranted into his right ear.

'Was I smiling?'

'Yes, you were! Why?'

'I'm always happy when I feel that I've got to the bottom

of things.' He still hadn't opened his eyes, which was making her even more furious because she felt as though she was talking to a brick wall endowed with vocal cords. She couldn't read what he was thinking from the expression in his eyes, and grappling with mere words was like trying to drink a glass of water with chopsticks.

'And you think you've got to the bottom of me, do you?' she spat out angrily. 'Despite what I say, you've assumed that I'm after marriage because you just can't tolerate the idea that a woman might politely decline an offer of a fling with you!'

'Yes, to the first part, and no, to the second.'

'And could you do me the courtesy of at least looking at me when we're having a conversation?'

He duly obliged and rested lazy, blue eyes on her flushed face.

'Better?' he enquired.

'Don't imagine that you can win me over with a little bit of charm,' she informed him tersely. 'I've made my mind up and I don't intend to change it. When we get back to London I shall see about finding somewhere else to live and...'

'Why?' he asked reasonably. 'You have my word that I won't pester you, so why worry to find somewhere else? You'll end up heavily out of pocket and you'll also leave Andy in the lurch. The poor boy won't know what to do if he's confined to the house with only his big brother for company.'

'You've been getting along much better recently,' Jade pointed out, sidetracked momentarily.

'But there's still a long way to go. We haven't really communicated for more years than I care to remember, and with all the best intentions in the world old habits die hard.'

What he said made sense. She could feel herself being

persuaded into staying put, at least for the moment. She could always dodge his company when he was around, and he wouldn't demand her presence at the dinner table or for drinks because he would know precisely why she wanted to avoid him...

'Besides...' He flicked a speck of non-existent fluff from his trousers and linked his fingers casually on his lap. His legs were spread slightly apart and his trousers had tightened over his muscular thighs. She made sure not to look too closely at the sight, just in case she became fixated and caught herself doing something crazy like tracing the contours of his legs through the material. To be on the safe side, she clasped her hands together and rooted them firmly on her lap.

'Besides...' he picked up, adjusting his legs a little further apart and this time resting his hand lightly on his thigh '...sooner or later my duties in England will come to an end, much to my regret...'

'You've enjoyed being back?' Diverted yet again.

'More than I thought. Funny thing is that I've spent so many years out of the country that I'd fancied myself as the ultimate cosmopolitan creature, but I guess I must just be a homebody after all.'

The thought of Curtis Greene being a homebody nearly brought on a laughing fit.

'But I won't be around for much longer...'

She hadn't considered that angle. She had thought about what it would feel like having to control her feelings in his company, listening from the haven of her bedroom for the sound of his car when he returned from work, for the click of the front door being opened and shut. She had imagined in rich detail the agony of hiding her love while her eyes struggled not to become entangled with his and her mind had fought furiously to break free of its leash. She hadn't thought about what it would feel like knowing that he was not around, that he had left the country and she would not set eyes on him again. The emptiness that rose in front of her was like the sudden vision of a black hole.

'I've more or less sorted out what needed to be sorted out. It's now just a matter of tying up a few loose ends and attending to the technicalities of who will replace Andy and in what capacity.'

She opened her mouth to say something nonchalant and cheerful on the subject and discovered that she couldn't speak. Her power of speech had been paralysed at the prospect of no longer being near him, whatever the circumstance.

'And, of course, I may just find someone else...' He let the words drop like poison between them, and then sighed laboriously.

Was it her imagination or were her facial muscles stiffening as well? She couldn't swallow! She blindly grabbed the glass of mineral water which had been poised, untouched, on the broad handrest, and gulped down a few mouthfuls.

'Just as you might...' he continued softly. 'Don't kid me by telling me that that vibrant, fiery, sexy, wanton woman I tasted and touched in Scotland is capable of going into hibernation again.'

Tasted...touched... The words evoked images of their lovemaking that were powerful enough to send a wave of moistness between her legs.

He leaned back against the seat, shut his eyes, and seemed perfectly satisfied to leave her with her conjurings.

And now that he had wrecked all her fragile stabs at self-control and determination, she found herself spending the remainder of the short flight in quiet, speechless panic at the prospect of loss. There were plenty of good, solid rea-

sons to combat the primitive terror she felt at losing him
completely and for ever, but could they make any head-
way? Could she feel even the vaguest glimmer of relief at
the thought of Curtis Greene going back to New York and
being out of her hair for good? She kept up a mental refrain
about time being the great healer, and tried to leapfrog the
present into some blissful point in the future when he would
be nothing more than a dim memory, but it was impossible.
The man kept rearing up into every scenario with the te-
nacity of an avenging angel.

It didn't help matters that he had now decided on polite
indifference to her, at her own miserable request.

They disembarked the plane in silence, and as soon as
they were outside he excused himself to make a phone call.

When he returned it was to inform her that he had to
leave immediately for a meeting in London.

And will I see you later? She wanted to ask. Instead she
nodded and looked away, squinting at the crowds.

'Don't expect me back tonight,' he added. 'So you can
breathe a sigh of relief, Jade.'

'I'm not relieved!' she countered, stoking up some of the
anger she had felt earlier on, because good, healthy rage
was better than this numbness that had settled in her blood-
stream like a toxin. 'Don't think for a moment...'

'This conversation has a *déjà vu* ring about it.' He looked
around, then glanced at his watch. 'And I just haven't got
the time to argue with you.' He rested his eyes on her face.
'Say hi to my brother.'

With that he was off in the opposite direction, cutting a
path through the crowds while she watched in rooted fascination as he weaved his way out of the airport foyer.
Before he reached the exit he turned and, mortified, Jade
realised that she had not left the spot. He had caught her

staring at him red-handed. So much for being cool and in charge of things.

She spun around and flounced away, only realising that she was heading in the wrong direction when she somehow found herself heading back towards the departure lounge, at which point she deftly manoeuvred herself towards the newsagents, bought herself a newspaper and retraced her steps towards the revolving exit doors.

Whatever snow had fallen on the streets of London had been trampled underfoot into muddy slush. It was much milder here than it had been in Scotland, and the threat in the air was of rain rather than snow. She managed to get a taxi and saw that everyone had their umbrellas at their sides, waiting for the inevitable downpour. The dreariness of it all made those few nights in Scotland, with its deep bed of pure white snow, even more magical in retrospect.

Good Lord, just what she needed! Mentally associating Curtis Greene with magic.

But magic, she thought wistfully, was what he had achieved, and in ways he would never have known. He had shown her joy and re-introduced her back into the land of the living. True, she had already taken the first few hesitant steps, but the ground she had covered with him had been more than a few steps. She had leapt forward. The over-whelming grief and guilt that had haunted her after her sister's condition had been diagnosed, that had plagued her all through her illness and hung on like a swollen leech after her death, had been put to rest. Her grief was easier to bear without the corresponding guilt. She could finally accept that Caroline had died, but that her death did not invalidate all the memories she, Jade, carried of her.

In a cruelly ironic way, the love that had blossomed for Curtis, futile as it was, had given her back her faith in life, had somehow counteracted the bitter sourness of the past.

It was as though she had been walking around for over two years without a soul, and he had returned hers, without even realising it.

She barely noticed when the taxi pulled up in front of the house, and she found that she couldn't wait to get back inside, back to the familiarity of her art things. Hopefully Andy would be around. She needed to talk to him. But as luck would have it, he was at college.

Restlessly she made herself a cup of coffee, settled down at the kitchen table and decided to continue with the project she had been working on before her trip to Scotland. It felt like a lifetime ago, and after staring down at the beautifully manicured but basically tame sketches, she ripped them into pieces, chucked the lot into the bin, pulled out a wad of fresh paper and began to draw.

The pencil flew across the paper as though possessed of a life of its own. Her previously neat, gorgeous and technically sound drawings were replaced by incisive strokes of sheer genius. Her portrait of the wicked rodent, Basil, took on undertones of cunning, and the timid rabbit, Daisy, was no longer merely timid but carried the promise of gritty courage in the wide eyes.

Sheet after sheet came alive. She made herself two more cups of coffee, stuck her feet on the kitchen table, rested the paper on her lap and failed to noticed time going by.

When it got dark, she switched on the kitchen light, absent-mindedly noticing that it was after five, and then lost herself again in her work. She had never felt inspired like this in her life before. It was as though a thousand feelings had been released and in the process some hidden but vital part of her creativity had been unblocked.

It occurred to her, when she paused for breath to look over the work she had done, that if she could maintain this frantic, inspired pace, then Curtis Greene's entrance into the twilit, manageable world of the 'Vaguely Remembered Though Not Entirely Forgotten' would be all the quicker.

She allowed optimism to flourish for a few seconds before sinking into blinding desolation, where she remained, staring vacantly at the kitchen wall, until she heard the clatter of footsteps, followed by a tousled, immensely cheerful-looking Andy.

'You're back!' he cried, whereupon she burst into immediate tears, and at five past seven was still at the kitchen table, attempting to regulate her puffy eyes and reddened, blotchy face into something resembling a human being.

'How could I have fallen in love with *your brother*?' she asked, for the umpteenth time. Before Andy could open his mouth, she stared past him, eyes narrowed, and glumly listed all the reasons that came to mind. 'Of course, I was stupid,' she dutifully reminded them both. 'I should have seen what was coming and got out while the going was good. How could I? *Your brother?* Someone I was *primed* to dislike! In fact, someone I *did* dislike! To start with...'

'Love is—'

'A nightmare.' Jade stood up and restlessly paced the kitchen, then slumped back into the chair and propped her chin in her hands. 'What about fairytale endings?' she demanded, leaning forward, palms flat on the table. 'You answer me that!'

'They don't—'

'Bloody exist!' She glared at Andy, who volunteered a rueful smile in return. 'He's *your* brother!' she accused.

'An accident of birth, darling. Nothing I can do about that!'

'I would never have set eyes on the man if it hadn't been for you...!'

'Oh, no, you don't!'

'Well,' she pouted sulkily, 'it's true! Besides, if you were a good enough friend, you'd give me free rein to vent all my frustrations on you.' But her vitriol had dissipated and they smiled feebly at one another. He was clasping her hand when they heard the front door slam and the sound of urgent footsteps heading towards the kitchen.

Guiltily, she snatched her hand back, just in time to see Curtis sweep through the door waving a newspaper in his hand.

He looked *something*, but she couldn't figure out what. Darkly flushed, energised, or maybe just terrifyingly sexy, with his top buttons undone and his free hand holding his jacket over his shoulder.

'Have either of you seen this?' He was still waving the newspaper and she wondered whether that look of his wasn't related to excessive drink. Why else would he be storming towards them flapping a newspaper in his hand? What was there to see in the newspaper? More updates on the Middle Eastern crisis? A further outbreak of Legionnaires' disease in some holiday resort? And was it *that* important? In her frame of mind, she hardly thought so.

He approached the table where she and Andy were still staring at him with twin expressions of bewilderment and slammed the paper onto the table.

'Look! Have a little read! Should get your appetites soaring!'

CHAPTER NINE

'BUT how on earth did this *happen*?' Jade demanded for the third time. She had stormed behind Curtis into the sitting room and now flounced into one of the chairs, tucking her feet underneath her and feverishly scanning the article again.

It was short and scandalously to the point. She and Curtis Greene, millionaire bachelor and fantasy of many an aspiring woman's dreams, were engaged. The article had been written with salacious gusto and listed the numerous dazzling women to whom he had been romantically linked over the years in America, including one very famous actress and an equally famous supermodel. In comparison, their succinct description of her, as an ordinary, run-of-the-mill art student, smacked of patronising incredulity, and she could understand why.

Andy, of course, had found the whole thing vastly amusing. He had been the first to snatch the newspaper out of his brother's hand, and she had left him in the kitchen gleefully quoting snippets of the article at her.

Scottish snow sends temperatures soaring...
    Jade Summers, mystery woman, manages to steal millionaire's heart...
    Former office worker and simple art student manages to net New York's biggest fish...
    Close friends say that this is the real thing...

'This is ridiculous!' she spluttered, staring at him while he calmly poured them both a drink. 'And I'm not in the

154

mood for a drink!' she flared, staring at the glass, then at his face, with tight-chested anger. 'And *what* friends? *What* close friends? Who are they talking about?'

'Drink it. Might calm you down.'

'I am perfectly calm!' she shouted back, and he shrugged, deposited the glass on the table next to her and then sat down on the sofa and languidly crossed his legs. He was a picture of self-control. The jacket had been discarded somewhere in the kitchen and he had roughly rolled the sleeves of his navy and blue pinstriped shirt to his elbows, affording her the unwelcome sight of his muscular arms sprinkled with dark hair.

She took a few deep breaths and leaned forward in the chair, resting the weight of her arms on her thighs.

'Do you have any idea how this ludicrous rumour started? It was one thing going along with a ridiculous, fictitious engagement in the middle of Scottish nowhere-land, but it's a different matter completely when it's splashed all over the gossip columns of the London newspapers!'

'I don't think Tom would be too impressed with your description of where he lives as "the middle of Scottish nowhere-land."'

'Stop trying to change the subject!'

'I'm merely trying to behave sensibly about this.'

'Behave sensibly?' Jade choked. '*Behave sensibly?* How can we behave sensibly when...when...?' Words nearly failed her. 'When...you fling a newspaper at me and I'm faced with my own name in print? Alongside yours? What,' she wailed, 'are we going to do?'

'Well,' he pointed out, swirling the glass around in his hand and then gulping down a generous mouthful, 'here's what we *can't* do. We can't take the article back.'

'Oh, that's very helpful!' Jade bit out sarcastically. 'Any more gems where that one came from?'

'And getting into a state about it isn't going to change that fact,' he carried on equably, as though she hadn't spoken. 'And spare a thought for *me*! What about *my* name? The City will be buzzing with this story by tomorrow morning. Business acquaintances will be phoning to find out whether the rumour's right or not! Not to mention all those leggy models and actresses who did their utmost to bring me to heel at the altar!' He grinned, and when he saw her thunderous expression said piously, 'According to the article.'

Jade decided that she needed that drink after all. She snatched the glass from the table, gulped down enough to steady her nerves, and afforded him a long, withering look. 'How did they get hold of this crazy story? If *you* hadn't seen fit to concoct the thing in the first place, we wouldn't be here now!'

'I didn't hear you bellowing the truth from all four corners at the time.'

'I *tried*, but you railroaded me into silence!'

'Ah! So it's all *my* fault now?'

'Yes.' She could say that without a flicker of conscience because from where she was sitting the whole mess *was* of his making. 'And you still haven't answered me. *How* did they get hold of our so-called engagement?'

He shrugged eloquently. 'Who knows? Maybe there was a reporter staying at Tom's place who recognised me and overheard the situation…'

'There were no reporters there.'

'How do you know? As far as I know, they don't have their occupation tattooed on their foreheads.'

Why, she thought sourly, wasn't he taking this seriously? *He* had more to lose than she had. She doubted any of her acquaintances would have come across the article, and if they had she would have no trouble shrugging the whole thing off as the usual fabricated journalism, too busy itching for a story to pay any attention to the truth. She had no family to telephone hurriedly and explain, and no close friends who might take mortal offence at being the last to know a succulent titbit. Curtis, on the other hand...

The thought bucked her up, because she knew that underneath the cool exterior he would be desperate to put any such tales of engagement to rest, especially ones linking him to Miss Average UK.

'I had no idea you were notorious enough to feature in *gossip columns*,' she informed him tartly.

Another expressive shrug. 'I'm rich, eligible, not yet decrepit...'

Jade's response was to toss the newspaper on the ground by the chair with scathing contempt. She shifted her legs from under her, wriggled her toes in their socks to get the blood circulation moving and adopted a more elegant pose with crossed legs and fingers linked primly on lap.

'Of course,' he mused, 'I'm more often featured in the business section...'

'Don't tell me. Because in addition to being blessed with looks and wealth, you're also razor-sharp in all known financial circles?'

He looked amazed that she had managed to spot the truth so quickly, and she clicked her tongue in irritation. What *she* personally found pretty stupendous was that nowhere in the article was his giant-sized ego mentioned. A huge oversight on their part, as far as she could see.

'There,' he said soothingly, 'didn't I tell you that a drink would help? You look a lot better now.'

Jade thought that what she could do with the remainder of her drink that would *really* help would be to fling it at his head. Instead, she reached over for the glass, drained the contents and felt pleasantly warm inside.

She decided that he had been right after all. No good getting hot under the collar over what was already in print. Let him find a way out of it. He wouldn't be so calm and collected when the implications of the story started hitting home. In fact, he hadn't looked nearly so cool an hour previously, when he had stormed into the kitchen waving the damned paper about like a demented preacher on his pulpit. Oh, no, it had been only her rattled overreaction that had served to calm him down, because his amusement at her response was greater than his worry over what had been written.

'So what are we going to do? Or perhaps I should say *you*. After all, as you correctly pointed out, *you're* going to be the one fending off all the nosy calls from ex-girlfriends and business chums.' She sat back with an expectant expression on her face. Expectant and superior, which was how she felt now that things had been put into perspective.

'Good question.' He appeared to give the dilemma a great deal of thought. Much frowning, narrowing of eyes, slight shakes of the head. Very ham actor, she thought, from her newly gained position of lofty indifference.

'What do *you* suggest…?'

'*I* don't care.'

'You don't?'

'No, I don't.' She flicked several non-imaginary specks of pastel sharpenings from her jeans and realised that not only were her fingers grubby from the colours but that her face would also bear the undignified and tell-tale signs of someone who had spent hours in front of paper using various charcoals, sketching pencils and oil pastels.

'Whether we're so-called engaged or not is no skin off

my nose! *I* won't be the one having to wriggle out of the lie. The people at art college don't tend to scour gossip columns in tabloids!' Put *that* in your pipe and smoke it, she thought with relish.

'It's *not*?'

'Nope. You forget, I don't *have* a reputation to consider. I'm invisible, whereas *you* are not.'

'Well, now, that puts a different complexion on things altogether.'

Jade, who had been on the verge of smacking her lips in sheer pleasure at the thought of seeing him wriggle like a worm on a hook, sat up a little straighter and frowned.

'What do you mean?'

'I mean it would actually suit my interests quite well at the moment to be engaged…'

'What?' Confusion brought a rush of hectic colour to her cheeks.

Curtis wasn't looking at her. He seemed to be ruminating, his mind a million miles away, his eyes half closed and speculative.

This was the last thing she had expected. Appalled horror, perhaps, but certainly not this.

'I'm in the middle of a very sensitive deal at the moment,' he said, thinking aloud. 'Japanese company.' He said this as though she should automatically follow his convoluted thought processes, and when she glowered at him with open incomprehension he continued to elaborate. 'Very big on honour,' he explained, getting up and flexing his muscles, then walking across to the concealed bar to pour himself another drink. 'Mr Akiyama, particularly, is very much the family man. He's made references to my bachelor state and my reputation as world-weary playboy with amiable acceptance, but I know he would feel easier at the thought of doing business with me if he knew that I was as much into family values as he is... Put it this way: he kind of sees this deal as one family firm doing business with another family firm...'

'That's ridiculous!'

'Who's to say what's ridiculous when it comes to another nation's culture?' Curtis said sanctimoniously.

'I mean,' Jade explained patiently, even though she felt on the verge of losing her rag altogether, 'it *makes no sense*. Are you telling me that huge Japanese companies refuse to do business with overseas firms unless they're headed by good, honest men with two point two children and a wife tidily at home keeping house?' She gave a snort of pure disbelief.

'Actually, his isn't a huge company. It's just vastly profitable.'

'Well, you'll have to find another fiancée for the job.'

'But I thought you said that it was no skin off your nose whether you were in print as being engaged to me or not.'

Jade stared at him speechlessly, stunned and amazed at the unexpected turn in the conversation. Just when she had managed to get her self-control into some sort of order and things had been rolling along in a pleasantly predictable fashion, with little left for her to do but watch as his smugness at dealing with the situation spilled over into dawning awareness of the messy inconvenience of something he had personally generated, whether he cared to admit it or not, she found that the rug had been yanked from under her feet.

It wasn't bloody fair! Hadn't he turned her life upside down enough already without enmeshing her further? She wanted to get him out of her system, not conspire to keep him there so that he could carry on choking up her arteries! From planning to leave his house the minute she got back to London, here she was, caught up in a charade which he was now proposing to prolong because it suited him!

'Maybe I misheard,' he offered, with an inclination of his head as he waited for her response.

'Maybe Mr…Mr…'

'Akiyama…?'

'…didn't read the article! It was only a few lines long…'

'Fifteen.'

'Do visiting Japanese pore over the gossip columns in tabloids when they're in a foreign language?'

He gave another of those galling *who knows?* shrugs. 'Even if he didn't, he deals with enough various people in the company to be filled in in no time at all. And I can tell you this: if I then have to launch into an explanation of the truth, with all its little twists and turns, then there'll be no deal.'

'But at least you wouldn't have lied to the man.'

'Only a small white lie.'

'A bloody whopper,' Jade broke in, in a raised voice.

'Besides, if we go along with it then the whole thing will subside into silence after a few days, and no more will be mentioned in the press on the subject. It'll all die a death. Be replaced by some other item of trivia that will capture the imagination. A week at the most and we can both retreat from an uncomfortable situation without having the need to deny anything.'

Jade fell back on telling him that the whole thing was ridiculous, but her voice sounded thin and unconvincing. Somehow she had managed to tie herself into knots, or rather she had let him tie her into knots without even realising it.

She remembered when they had been at Tom's, the overt touching that had been done to make their little white lie more convincing. She imagined Curtis touching her again, as another charade was enacted, and to her dismay found that the thought was more palatable than the prospect, which she had faced in the past day, of never seeing him again.

'I shall be having dinner with Mr Akiyama and his wife tomorrow evening,' he said smoothly. 'Naturally they would be delighted to see you. And we can take things from there…'

'Take things from there…where to?'

The situation now seemed to be moving along with bewildering speed. Her heart was knocking against her ribcage and she could feel the blood rushing around in her veins.

'One or two client dinners…'

'I thought you said that in a week the whole thing could be swept under the carpet…'

'In a week the public will have forgotten about us. As far as business acquaintances go it may take a little longer…'

Jade's eyes widened into unfocused alarm. Path One, which she had envisaged earlier and which had seen him leaving the country for good, had now been joined by Path Two, which saw them thrown together in an awkward pretence for the sake of outside eyes. Which of the two alternatives was worse?

In her heart, she knew which one, but she resolutely fought down the desire to submit to his plan even though she knew that she had stupidly talked herself into it in the first place.

'We'll have to get a ring,' he said, breaking into her tormented thoughts with an observation that had her snapping hurriedly back to the present at the speed of light.

'What for? I didn't wear one in Scotland.'

'Because Tom knows me,' he said, in a voice that implied that no further explanation was deemed necessary. 'But...'

'But a ring...?' she croaked.

'Nothing too elaborate,' he soothed. 'Just some old family heirloom...'

'Old family heirloom?' Wasn't that the definition of 'elaborate'?

'You look a bit green round the gills,' he said, concerned. 'Better have a bit more of that drink of yours.'

Obediently, Jade gulped down the rest. Two strong gin and tonics, a drink she was quite unaccustomed to having, and things shifted obligingly into some kind of perspective, twisted though it was.

'Why do I get the feeling that I've been manipulated?' she asked gloomily. The alcohol had taken the edge off her fire. Now she was simmering away gently and was dismayed to discover that the thought of a couple of weeks in Curtis's company, far from filling her with dread, gave her an illicit thrill. As though she had somehow bought time, even though common sense repeated what it had initially told her, that buying time with Curtis Greene was not a good idea. She would only pay for it later.

If he had never mentioned the fact that he would be leaving the country for good, it would never have occurred to her that what she really needed was to get her fill of him before he left. That simple aside, and all its nightmarish sense of accompanying loss, had been sufficient to shift the emphasis of her emotional state from determined into desperate. Or so it seemed, as she absent-mindedly took a third glass from him. At least this one, she thought, sipping at it, was half the strength of the previous two. On the fringes of her mind she wondered whether he had been mixing these drinks particularly strong so that he could verbally

outwit her, but the thought was so silly that she shoved it
back into immediate obscurity.

She would enjoy the next week or so, savour the treacherous thrill of being in Curtis's company even if it *was*
under false pretences, and, since her heart was as in deep
as it could get, it surely couldn't do much more to her frame
of mind.

How wrong that logically argued illusion turned out to
be.

Dinner with Mr Akiyama and his wife turned out to be
a mere taster of how Curtis's presence could knock her for
six.

There was no overdone touching, no romantic whispers
into her ear, but enough brooding, steamy looks to send her
pulses soaring, and at the end of the evening, when his
fingers intimately traced the contours of her spine through
her dress, she found herself having to prop herself against
the doorframe to shake her host's hand as they said goodbye. The taxi ride back was an agony of wanting that had
her bolting to her bedroom just to try and escape.

Then came a series of client dinners. His social calendar
seemed suddenly full to bursting point, and her days took
on the heightened hue of someone living in a rarefied atmosphere. Away from the public eye he was the model of the
perfect gentleman, allowing her all the freedom she wanted
to dodge, keeping his distance, at least physically, although
his charm and wit reluctantly forced a response out of her
whenever they found themselves alone together.

In company, it was a different matter. He was not averse
to being shockingly suggestive in his attentiveness. Every
touch made nonsense of her nightly litany to call the whole
thing a day. On two occasions, when the client functions
were held in the less formal arena of one of London's select
clubs that featured music and dancing, they danced to-

gether, their bodies sinuously entwined, his hand pressing into the small of her back while their legs, moving as one, generated enough erotic images in her head to bring her to the point of collapse.

They were now into week three, and their social agenda showed little sign of diminishing. Tonight they were going to supper with four business associates. Smart but casual. She was now dressed, smartly but casually, in a figure-hugging heather-coloured wool dress which skimmed her thighs and, with high shoes, made her legs look longer than they were. She had already shamefully acknowledged to herself that she was beginning to get a taste for dressing up and socialising, two things she had never had much interest in.

More than once it had occurred to her that that was simply because with Curtis around the simplest and most tedious of events became a playground of furtive looks and weak but thrilling craving. Her body trembled like a leaf in a breeze every time he touched it, even though his touching was confined to public places, and to that, too, she was becoming addicted. Too late, now, to try and stop the rollercoaster ride. But she wasn't sleeping with him. She had stayed true to those principles, if nothing else.

He had told her that he would fetch her at eight-thirty promptly, and she was waiting for him in the hall when she heard his key being inserted into the lock.

He opened the door and looked at her for a few seconds, his body perfectly still.

'That's new, isn't it? The colour suits you.'

Jade didn't know what to say to this, so to fill in the embarrassed silence she reverted to her old friend, the frown.

'Where are we going tonight?' Ignore compliment, something she specialised in, was next on the menu, but disturbingly he walked into the hall and closed the door behind him.

'Nowhere. We're eating in. I've brought a Chinese take-away.'

'But I thought you said that...' she began, floundering nervously at this change of events.

'We were going to be wining and dining with my associates, but I cancelled it.' He produced a bag from behind him like a magician producing a rabbit from a hat. 'In favour of something a little less strenuous.' He divested himself of his jacket and began loosening his tie, undoing the top buttons of his shirt, rolling up the sleeves. Jade watched his movements with the fascination of someone being hypnotised.

'I think it's time we talked,' he said quietly. He looked at her so intently that her nerves stretched like taut elastic into panic.

'What about?' she squeaked.

'Us.'

This was the beginning of the end. She could feel it in her bones. After the whirl of social events, they would now conveniently begin tapering off, and finally he would be able to say that things just hadn't worked out. The Japanese deal had been done. She was now surplus to requirements. The cold fear which had gripped her when she had first faced the prospect of his departure returned with renewed vigour, thrilled to be back in the game.

'What about us?'

'Not here.' He nodded towards the kitchen and she trailed behind him, heart pounding like a sledgehammer, watching in silence as he removed little boxes from the bag and fetched a couple of plates from the cupboard.

He helped himself to food. She helped herself to some orange stuff, some noodle-looking stuff and some brown stuff with bits of green thrown in. When she began eating, it all tasted like cardboard.

'How have you enjoyed the past few weeks?' he asked, when he was into his third mouthful of food.

'Fine.' For someone, she thought, who had been living on borrowed time.

He didn't answer for a while, just carried on eating, then he looked at her over his chopsticks.

'I thought so too.'

'Better make sure no one knows that.' She laughed, with an edge of hysteria in her voice. 'Not if the intention is to ease them in gently to the inevitable breakdown of our relationship.' She laughed again, and this time she could detect definite mania in the laugh. Oh, God. That had to stop.

'Which brings me to the essence of what I have to say.' He looked so *serious*. Why did he have to look so serious? Why couldn't he reduce the whole thing to light-hearted banter? Couldn't he see how close she was to tears? She closed her chopsticks, neatly lining them up in perfect parallels, and tried to clear her face of all emotion.

'Which is?'

'That I think we should make this legal.'

The bottom seemed to drop out of her world. One minute her stomach was churning in anticipation of the worst, the next minute she had no stomach. It had shot downwards at speed. 'Legal?' she asked weakly.

'Get married. Tie the knot. Call it what you want.' He stood up and began clearing the table, and she hastily followed, both working in silence and avoiding eye contact.

'I mean,' he continued, dumping his plate in the sink, 'as far as teams go, we make a pretty good one.' He still wasn't looking at her. 'Everyone's taken to you, even some of my more forthright, obnoxious clients. You've charmed the lot of them. They all think that you're fresh and young and invigorating.'

And what do you think?

'None of this love business to complicate matters.' Scrape, scrape, scrape as congealing food hit the bin liner.

You don't love me. Why not just say it?

'You could carry on with your art course, naturally. There would be a lot of entertaining were I to remain here permanently.' The clatter of plates being washed, drowning out his voice. Still no eye contact.

Are you embarrassed to look me in the face because you're ashamed of turning the institution of marriage into a business arrangement, or do you just want to avoid my eyes in case I give in to an outpouring of horrid, nasty, unwelcome emotion?

'So what do you say?' His back to her as he vigorously scrubbed plates clean and stuck them onto the draining board.

She unglued her tongue from the roof of her mouth and heard herself say,

'Can I think about it?'

'That's the worst bit,' she confessed four hours later to Andy.

Sleep, after that surreal conversation, had eluded her, and she had crept into Andy's room, in her nightie, and was now sitting cross-legged on his bed, pouring out her heart. What would she do without him?

'He doesn't love me, he made that fact perfectly clear, yet instead of throwing his ridiculous proposal back into his face I ended up asking him if *I could think about it*! Am I mad, Andy? Do I look like a lunatic to you? Why am I behaving like one?'

'You've now been bending my ear for...' he glanced at

his bedside clock '...forty minutes, darling, and you still won't say it, will you?'

'Say *what*?'

'That, love or no love, you want to marry my brother.'

Jade shot him one long, telling, forlorn look, then sidled up to him without unfolding her legs and sank into him. 'Oh, God,' she moaned, 'Ohgoddogoddogoddogod. I'm an utter fool. I could give lectures on stupidity. I'm totally and irretrievably insane. I *want* to marry for love. I *want* violins and promises of a wonderful ever after, but, failing that, I just want to spend the rest of my life with your damned brother. Tell me I'm an idiot. Please? Better still, tell me that there's some pill I can take to get back to normal. I keep thinking that I could convince him that I'm indispensable, that he loves me after all, even if he seems to have chucked in the whole sex bit without too much looking back.'

Andy didn't answer. He just stroked her hair, which was what she needed, and gradually she began to feel a bit calmer. She had talked herself out and now the only talking going on was in her head. The word *fool* was cropping up a great deal, coupled with *madwoman* and *misguided idiot*. She was beginning to be lulled into a light sleep, and was gearing herself to get back to her own bed, when the bedroom door was pushed open and they both looked in unison to see Curtis standing on the threshold, his face dark with rage. Thunderous with rage, in fact. Ten seconds of complete silence turned into several hours as six eyes tangled, then Jade let out a squeal of horror and leapt from the bed, as though the mattress had suddenly gone up in flames.

In that minuscule space of time Curtis had turned away, slamming the door behind him. The noise reverberated through the silent house like a clap of thunder. Jade acted on instinct. She glanced back at Andy, only to wave him back into bed because he seemed on the verge of following her, then she was running, nightie flying around, pelting towards Curtis's bedroom, banging on the door, determined that he would open it if she had to keep up the assault for the next two hours.

She wanted him. Yes, she did. Wanted him enough to take him even though she knew that he didn't love her. Wanted him enough to suffer a lifetime of unrequited love in return for his presence in her life.

It only occurred to her after several minutes of banging to try the door handle, and it turned easily. He hadn't locked the door!

He was standing by the window, staring out, and he didn't turn when she padded into the bedroom.

'How long?' was the only thing he said as she approached him, tentatively reaching out to put her hand on his arm but letting it drop to her side instead.

'There's nothing going on…'

'Don't lie to me.' His voice was low, even and chillingly controlled. 'When did you and Andy devise your little plan for you to get me into bed so that my money could join the nest egg? Has he gone through his inheritance, or maybe greed took over somewhere along the line…when the opportunity presented itself? Was that why you were so adamant about not becoming my mistress? Holding out for the big thing?' He finally turned around to face her, and his face was as chillingly controlled as his voice had been. 'I should have suspected something, but you both carried off the "just friends" act so convincingly that I actually believed you.' His mouth twisted into a sneer of pure dislike and she flinched as though he had struck her.

'You don't understand…'

'*What* don't I understand?'

She looked at him blindly, unable to continue. Keeping

silent now was the end of all her meagre hopes, but silence was the one thing she had to maintain. She owed it to Andy.

'You don't understand,' she whispered. Just when she wanted to catch his eye, he turned away.

'Pack your bags tomorrow and leave this house, and you can tell my brother to do the same. If either of you ever dares set foot in it again I'll have the police throw you out. Now get out.'

'But, please…' She was pleading now, and the first tear had splashed down her cheek. 'You *don't understand*. There's nothing between me and Andy…'

'Because, big brother,' came a voice from the doorway, 'I'm gay.'

CHAPTER TEN

AS BOMBSHELLS went, that one could have stopped a charging rhino at ten paces.

Jade had not known what to expect. Fury, outrage, disgust, according to Andy and his busy imagination. In all events, the one reaction she had not anticipated was the one reaction that Curtis had afforded her. Surprise, yes, but then that had been swiftly followed by calm acceptance. She wished that Andy had had the courage to stay and witness his brother's reaction for himself, but, having finally confessed his bitter secret, he had swept out of the room and out of the house like a vacating tornado.

They had both heard the sound of his steps clattering down the stairs, then the distant slam of the front door.

Now Curtis was sitting in the paisley-covered stiff chair by the bay window of his bedroom. He was far too big for it, but for once his restless energy seemed to be dormant. His legs were extended straight in front of him and his hands hung over the sides of the chair. He looked like a giant who had decided to appropriate a chair designed for a midget.

Jade had retreated warily to the other side of the room onto the sofa, which she had had to clear of discarded ties, several business magazines and, incongruously, a silk bathrobe which had been carelessly slung over the arm.

For the past ten minutes she had watched and left him to his thoughts. She would have given a million dollars to crawl inside his head and find out first-hand what he was

172

thinking, but as it was she had to content herself with second-guessing.

It only occurred to her when he finally stood up that he might not have wanted her around, might *still* not want her around now, that her presence might be intrusive at a time when he might need privacy to contemplate revelations which had been a long time coming, and she hesitantly stood up as well, uneasily aware that she should have had the foresight to leave at the same time as Andy, instead of hanging around like a spare part. All the things she had been bursting to say since she had stormed into his bedroom carrying her banner of self-righteous self-defence had vanished with Andy's confession.

'Where are you going?' he asked. She realised, with a start, that those were the first words he had spoken for the past ten minutes.

'I thought...' she mumbled, spreading her hands in a helpless gesture, '...that perhaps you might want some time to yourself to...you know...think about...you know...' It occurred to her that Curtis Greene had the amazing ability to reduce her vocabulary to stuttering, inarticulate nonsense, someone in desperate need of English lessons.

'What's there to think about?' he answered smoothly. 'Sit back down.'

She obeyed without thinking, and he strolled over to where she was sitting and flopped onto the sofa next to her.

'You could have told me from the very beginning,' he said, 'when I first accused you of having an affair with my brother. Why didn't you?'

It was a very small two-seater sofa. He had extended his arm along the back and his fingertips were close enough to touch her hair. His legs were inches away from hers. It was certainly not the place to have an impartial conversation about anything, at least not for her, when half her mind was preoccupied with his proximity. The fact that the room was lit only by the two bedside lamps made the atmosphere all the more hazardous to her nervous system.

'Because it was up to your brother to…finally confront you…explain…whatever you want to call it…'

'Everything slots into place now,' he murmured, and the low throb of his voice wrapped itself around her like a blanket.

'What? *What* everything?'

'Fragments of the past.' He sighed. 'Too late to say that I wish he had confided in me sooner.'

'How could he? You were never around.'

'No,' he admitted ruefully. 'I really never was.'

'Too busy pursuing your own life,' she said on a little sigh of her own, and he didn't argue the point. Instead, to her dismay, he touched a strand of her hair, then withdrew his hand almost immediately, before she could pull back.

'What were you discussing with him that couldn't wait until morning?' he asked ruminatively. 'Was it us?'

He wasn't going to discuss Andy, and she respected him for that. Later they would talk, as brothers, with no areas left uncovered, but for now he had other things on his mind. She flushed guiltily and recovered some of her lost spark.

'*Us?* There *is* no ''us''.'

'Oh, yes, there is. Very much so, and there's no point denying it any longer.'

She wished that he would use his normal voice, instead of this low, seductive drawl that had her mesmerised. She imagined her eyeballs spinning around in circles, like a figure out of a cartoon, and almost smiled at the image.

Another passing touch of her hair, just a whisper of a touch as his finger brushed across her forehead, leaving a tingling feeling where it had been.

'If you weren't talking to Andy about us, then what were

you talking to him about?' he persisted, not letting her off the hook. Her eyes darted to his, and darted away, unable to withstand the brooding intensity in his gaze.

'Art.'

'At *that* hour of the night?' He laughed, amused and disbelieving, and she glared ferociously at him in response. 'Pull the other one.'

'The world, believe it or not, Curtis Greene, does *not* revolve around *you*. Conversations can be generated about any number of things in which you don't feature.' He was still smiling at her, and she wished that she could think of something pithy that would wipe the smile off his face. She knew how he was interpreting events, throwing her into the role of emotionally hijacked woman who was so consumed with passion for him that she had to pour her poor little heart and soul out to someone in the middle of the night.

'And why did *you* storm out when you saw us together?' she threw at him, taking random aim and unconsciously hitting the right target. 'Were you *jealous*?'

The sudden dark flush that spread across his cheeks was answer enough, and she was momentarily silenced by it. Silence was dangerous though. Even as dangerous as his nearness, because it emphasised the frantic beat of her heart and tightened the tension between them until she could almost hear her nerves beginning to shred.

'Would you believe me if I told you that I was?'

'Yes,' Jade answered promptly. 'I'm sure you would be, because you don't mind letting go. You just find it galling if the tables are turned.' She expected to find some answering glimmer of assent in his eyes, but instead she saw nothing. He just continued to stare at her, as though he wanted to eat her up with his eyes. It gave her the most peculiar sensation. One of being possessed. She wasn't sure that she liked it. Possession was too closely linked with lust, as far as she could see, and lust was the thing that had ended up coming between them and turning her world on its head.

'You're right. I was jealous. In fact, I wanted to rip his legs and arms off.'

Jade squirmed in the face of this raw, naked emotion. No, she was not going to let herself be persuaded by it. No, she was certainly not going to get turned on by it. In fact, she *ordered* her body to listen to her brain, but the sudden heavy ache in her breasts and the throbbing in her groin was evidence that her body, as usual, had decided to go its own way, irrespective of her commands.

She licked her lips nervously and let her eyes slide away from his, down to the carpet, where they remained fixed and unseeing.

'Jealousy is a very unhealthy emotion,' she muttered thickly, kicking her bare toe into the carpet and watching it deepen the colour of the pelt.

'It certainly would have been if I'd followed my instincts, but I didn't. Shall I tell you something?'

He was doing it again. Stroking her hair. She shifted slightly, but his fingers followed the movement of her body and she lacked the will to pull away again. She liked him doing that. She *liked* him touching her. Wasn't that why she had spent an hour with Andy, verbalising all the reasons why she couldn't go through with the marriage arrangement he had proposed? Because she had hoped that hearing her reasons spoken out loud might convince her that the thread of temptation snaking through her was a lost cause?

'What?' she heard herself ask.

'It was something of a relief.'

'What was?' Her eyes inched away from the fascinating sight of her toes to the bottoms of his trousers. If they travelled much further they would hit his thighs. She kept them firmly rooted to his calves.

'Andy's passionate declaration.' He laughed drily. 'The first thing that ran through my head when he said it was *Thank God*. I've never quite been able to erase the image of the two of you in bed watching television at eleven in the evening when that leak occurred.'

'So now you know.'

'So now I do,' he agreed absently. 'Look at me. I don't like addressing the side of your face, ravishing though your profile might be.'

'Why are you doing this?' she whispered, dragging her eyes to meet his.

'What?'

'Being like this, when...'

'I'm being honest with you. Don't you want my honesty?'

'You're playing with me.'

'Oh, no, I'm not, my girl.' He laughed softly under his breath, as though amused at something that had suddenly occurred to him. 'I can show you what it's like to be played with, if you want.' Without waiting for her response, he curled one loop of her hair around his finger and gently pulled her towards him, then he bent across and trailed his tongue over her mouth. 'That's playing,' he murmured huskily. 'Does it feel good? Would you like me to play with you some more?'

She had thought that he had given up trying to get her into bed, that he respected her reasons for refusing him and had turned on the charm to suit the occasion, in accordance with their little spate of play acting. She realised now that he had simply been biding his time, waiting in the wings. She had left him wanting her, and Curtis Greene always got what he wanted.

His finger trailed the side of her face, then the column of her neck, then her collarbone, dipping provocatively to the neckline of her baggy tee shirt which she was wearing as a nightdress.

'You have to stop being so afraid,' he said in a low voice, thick and velvety and disarmingly soft. 'You have to stop pulling away.'

'And you have to start remembering that people have feelings!' she burst out, blushing with dismay as she heard the words resound through the room like bullets from a gun.

'What do you think I'm talking about?'

Jade was confused. She didn't like the way he was looking at her, as though he was privy to some piece of knowledge that she wasn't. His wayward hand now discovered the new, bare territory of her thighs, which the tee shirt only partially covered, despite her attempts to stretch it down.

'I've spent the past few weeks humouring you,' he murmured roughly, 'and I think it's time to call it a day.'

'Humouring me? *Humouring me?*' she squeaked, outraged and mystified. The offending thigh, meanwhile, had been lulled into a delicious state of security and was resisting all attempts at movement. He stroked it and looked at her intently. She ignored the stroking and returned his gaze without flinching. Transfixed as she was by this weird conversation, she wasn't so transfixed that her mind couldn't amble off down a side road and window-shop in the place labelled 'How Would It Feel If His Hand Stole Up A Little Higher?'

'I was willing to wait for you to work through your problems.'

'Work through my problems?'

'Stop repeating everything I say. You're beginning to sound like a parrot.'

'Can I help it? Can I?' Jade demanded. 'Nothing you're saying makes any *sense*. What do you mean *you were willing to wait for me to work through my problems*?'

'I knew you were afraid of involvement,' he said slowly. His hand had crept a little higher and she felt the breath catch in her throat. 'And I don't blame you. I knew it the minute I laid eyes on you, and the more I looked at you, the stronger the feeling got. Half of you wanted me; the other half wanted to run away. When you told me about your sister, it all made sense.'

She didn't like where this was heading. Oh, no. She had never confessed any of that stuff to him. How did he know?

Because, a little voice whispered, he knew *her*.

'I think we should stop this right here and now,' she said in a timid, small voice which he didn't appear to hear at all.

'But I need to know your decision. Are you going to marry me or not? If we marry, then I stay here, but in the meantime there are appointments waiting to be made upon my departure.' His hand slipped underneath the tee shirt, caressing her waist, and she made a feeble attempt to still it, which unfortunately left it painfully close to her breasts, inches away from the soft mound of flesh and nipples that had tightened in response to his touch.

'Why me?' she asked, skirting round the question rather skilfully, she considered. 'London is full of young girls who would love to play hostess to your dinner parties. Why not go and fish one of *them* out of obscurity and offer her the job?'

'Because, if you really want to know, I'm not interested in taking any of them to bed. In fact, I've discovered that I'm not interested in taking *anyone* to bed apart from you.'

'So we're back to *that*, are we?' she asked, bristling.

'No, we're back to something quite different. A marriage proposal.'

'Arrangement, you mean.'

'Will you marry me?'

'Because you want to take me to bed? That's quite a big price to pay for sleeping with someone you'll grow sick of within months, isn't it?' It felt good to punish herself for wanting his hand where it was, for wanting it to go further and further and further, for wanting to marry this man when every instinct told her to back off.

'Not too big a price to pay for someone who's in love with me.'

It took a few seconds for the words to hit home, but when they did her body jerked back as though scalded. His hand, comfortably but motionlessly resting on her skin, became tangled with her tee shirt, and as soon as it was free she drew her legs up, enfolding them with the flimsy cotton.

'What gives you the idea that…that…?' She choked on a laugh. 'You're mad if you think that…that…'

'Just say it.'

'I suppose you think that you're holding a trump card, don't you?' she yelled, swinging her legs off the sofa and standing up. She angled away from him, bumping into a chest of drawers and righting her position without taking her eyes off his face. 'I suppose you think that you can finally have what you want! Just because I happen to have been stupid and insane enough to have made the mistake of falling in love with you, you imagine that you can now just talk me into getting into bed with you! Well, let me tell you something, buster. I might have climbed into the sack with you if I *didn't* love you! Hah! *Now* do you think you've been clever? Yes, I love you, and that's precisely why I don't intend to sleep with you and I certainly don't intend to marry you!'

Earlier temptation had been tossed through the window. In her humiliation and rage, she couldn't imagine how on earth she could ever have contemplated bending to his persuasion. She must have been even crazier than she imagined!

'I suppose you do this all the time, do you? Seduce women and then make them fall for you hook, line and sinker? Gives you some kind of sick kick, does it?' She paused for breath and folded her arms belligerently across her chest, arching her body forward as though gearing up to run full head-on tilt at him. 'You're forever talking to me about challenges...challenges, challenges, challenges! Is *that* your ultimate challenge? Worming your way under a woman's skin until she can't think of anyone but you, and then discarding her like an old shoe that no longer has a use in the wardrobe? Is that how you get your thrills?'

She was yelling so loudly that she was pretty sure her voice was tearing through the closed door, down the hall and straight into Andy's room. If he hadn't stormed out of the house he would probably have been charging right now into the bedroom at the thought of imminent homicide. She couldn't help it, though. Her emotions were so big and wild and bloody furious that she couldn't have modulated her tone if she'd tried. It didn't help that Curtis wasn't shouting back.

He stood up and walked across to her. Fisticuffs! If he so much as uttered one laugh of derision, he would discover the meaning of the word. She balled her hands into tight fists and every muscle in her body tensed to receive some awful body blow.

He was smiling, a slow, gentle smile that she distrusted, even though the messages flying to her brain were confusingly urging her to respond.

'This,' he murmured, putting his arms around her, wrapping himself around her, 'is why I love you so much. You're so utterly unpredictable and fragile and passionate and everything else that would take far too long for me to put into words. Aside from which...' he bent slightly so that he was whispering directly into her ear '...I don't have the vocabulary.'

For the space of a heartbeat time stood still, then she said in a high, wobbly voice, 'I don't believe you.'

'Put your arms around me, little darling.'

She did. But tentatively. 'I still don't believe you.' But was she mistaken? He was stroking her hair in a very tender manner and she could feel him kissing the top of her head.

'Why did you let me rant and rave? Why didn't you just tell me from the start and save me the mortification...?'

'Because I wasn't sure if you would rush in with accusations of saying the right thing just to get you into bed or persuade you into marriage because it happened to suit me. You don't stop to think, do you...?' He pushed her away from him so that he could tilt her face up to his and look at her.

'I think I fell in love with you long before we went to Scotland, even though I hadn't come close to admitting it to myself. Life as a bachelor was easy. I didn't intend to give it up without a fight. I certainly never entertained the idea that I would become so fixated with a woman that I'd end up doing everything in my power to keep her by my side. I knew you felt *something* for me, but I also knew that it wouldn't take much to have you running in the opposite direction so fast I'd never be able to catch you. I knew that I had to proceed cautiously, like someone defusing a bomb...'

'Does that mean you see me as a bombshell?' she asked, fully relaxed, her arms holding him tightly. She felt blissfully happy. It was a state of mind she had never known existed, and she figured that she could grow accustomed to it without too much difficulty.

'Absolutely.' He grinned at her, and she grinned stupidly back.

'I wish you'd said something sooner,' she murmured.

'I didn't want to make sweeping declarations of love any more than you did. Strong, powerful and dynamic as I am, I *do* still have an inherent teenage fear of the rebuff, you know.'

He smiled wickedly at her and her loving fingers crept to the waistband of his trousers and inserted themselves underneath, then swivelled to the front and casually undid the button of the trousers. She could feel him pulsing against her, but she was in no hurry. They had all the time in the world.

'When you said that you intended to move out of the house as soon as we returned to London from Scotland, I was so bloody terrified that I did the unthinkable. Having spent years loathing the intrusion of the media into my private life, I telephoned a journalist friend and told him that I was engaged.'

'You didn't!' She was so stunned by this announcement that she repeated, 'You didn't!' in sheer amazement.

'I was desperate!' he told her sheepishly. 'I wanted to buy time, so that I could try and find out exactly what you felt and give you time to come to terms with whatever you were feeling.'

'And if I'd decided that I wasn't ready to feel anything...?' She batted her eyelashes teasingly.

'Got something in your eye?'

'I'm being cute and kittenish.' She pouted for good measure, and he bent and kissed her thoroughly on the lips.

'Such a turn-on,' he murmured against her mouth, and

he scooped her up, giggling like a teenager, and deposited her firmly in the centre of the bed.

'Okay,' he said, disengaging himself from his clothes, which he carelessly tossed on the floor, then beginning work on her—not that there was much needed. A tee shirt hardly involved much effort. 'The big question.' He pulled her to his side and ran his hand smoothly along her thigh, then between her thighs, finding her wetness and massaging her there until she groaned and could hardly think, never mind answer any big questions.

'Um,' she murmured, parting her legs and moving her body sinuously against his hand.

'Will you marry me?'

'On one condition,' she whispered huskily, stretching back and linking her fingers above her head so that her breasts pointed provocatively at him.

'And what's that…?'

'That you never stop doing this.'

He bent his head to suckle on one nipple, then turned to look at her.

'I think—' he licked her nipple '—it's safe to say—' he nuzzled against it, pulling it into his mouth '—there's no chance of that…my love…'

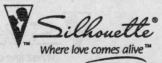

MAITLAND MATERNITY

MAITLAND MATERNITY

Where the luckiest babies are born!

In July 2001, look for

A DAD AT LAST

by Marie Ferrarella

Could Connor O'Hara possibly turn into a family man?

Connor O'Hara had a family now. At least, he had a son.
And a mother. And a whole mess of relatives he hadn't even
known were his close kin.

And then there was Lacy. Sweet Lacy Clark. Who'd suffered so
much for bringing little Chase, his son, into the world.

Frankly, it was all too much to take in for a guy used to being a loner,
to belonging nowhere, to living life on his own terms. In his heart,
he knew Lacy wanted the fairy tale, the white picket fence,
the whole nine yards. But really, he was having trouble
right now giving her even an inch!

Silhouette®
Where love comes alive™

HARLEQUIN®
Makes any time special ™

REGENCY
ROMANCE

Visit the elegant English countryside,
explore the whirlwind of London Society
and meet feisty heroines who tame roguish
heroes with their wit, zest and feminine
charm in...The Regency Collection.

Available in July 2001 at your favorite retail outlet:

THE LARKSWOOD LEGACY
by Nicola Cornick

MISS JESMOND'S HEIR
by Paula Marshall

A KIND AND
DECENT MAN
by Mary Brendan

AN INDEPENDENT LADY
by Julia Byrne

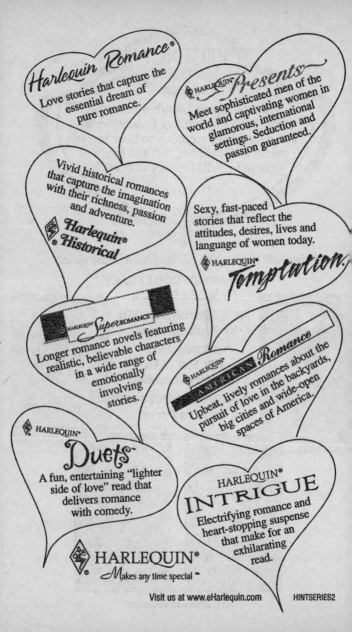

Harlequin Romance®
Love stories that capture the essential dream of pure romance.

HARLEQUIN Presents~
Meet sophisticated men of the world and captivating women in glamorous, international settings. Seduction and passion guaranteed.

Vivid historical romances that capture the imagination with their richness, passion and adventure.
Harlequin® Historical

Sexy, fast-paced stories that reflect the attitudes, desires, lives and language of women today.
HARLEQUIN® Temptation.

HARLEQUIN SuperRomance®
Longer romance novels featuring realistic, believable characters in a wide range of emotionally involving stories.

HARLEQUIN® AMERICAN Romance
Upbeat, lively romances about the pursuit of love in the backyards, big cities and wide-open spaces of America.

HARLEQUIN® Duets™
A fun, entertaining "lighter side of love" read that delivers romance with comedy.

HARLEQUIN® INTRIGUE
Electrifying romance and heart-stopping suspense that make for an exhilarating read.

HARLEQUIN®
Makes any time special™

Harlequin truly does make any time special.... *This year we are celebrating weddings in style!*

To help us celebrate, we want you to tell us how wearing the Harlequin wedding gown will make your wedding day special. As the grand prize, Harlequin will offer one lucky bride the chance to **"Walk Down the Aisle"** in the Harlequin wedding gown!

There's more...

For her honeymoon, she and her groom will spend five nights at the **Hyatt Regency Maui.** As part of this five-night honeymoon at the hotel renowned for its romantic attractions, the couple will enjoy a candlelit dinner for two in Swan Court, a sunset sail on the hotel's catamaran, and duet spa treatments.

A HYATT RESORT AND SPA   Maui • Molokai • Lanai

To enter, please write, in, 250 words or less, how wearing the Harlequin wedding gown will make your wedding day special. The entry will be judged based on its emotionally compelling nature, its originality and creativity, and its sincerity. This contest is open to Canadian and U.S. residents only and to those who are 18 years of age and older. There is no purchase necessary to enter. Void where prohibited. See further contest rules attached. Please send your entry to:

Walk Down the Aisle Contest

In Canada	In U.S.A.
P.O. Box 637	P.O. Box 9076
Fort Erie, Ontario	3010 Walden Ave.
L2A 5X3	Buffalo, NY 14269-9076

You can also enter by visiting www.eHarlequin.com
Win the Harlequin wedding gown and the vacation of a lifetime!
The deadline for entries is October 1, 2001.

HARLEQUIN®
Makes any time special ®

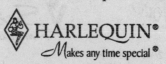